THE
DEADLIER SEX

Randy Wayne White
writing as Randy Striker

A SIGNET BOOK

SIGNET
Published by New American Library, a division of
Penguin Group (USA) Inc., 375 Hudson Street,
New York, New York 10014, USA
Penguin Group (Canada), 90 Eglinton Avenue East, Suite 700, Toronto,
Ontario M4P 2Y3, Canada (a division of Pearson Penguin Canada Inc.)
Penguin Books Ltd., 80 Strand, London WC2R 0RL, England
Penguin Ireland, 25 St. Stephen's Green, Dublin 2,
Ireland (a division of Penguin Books Ltd.)
Penguin Group (Australia), 250 Camberwell Road, Camberwell, Victoria 3124,
Australia (a division of Pearson Australia Group Pty. Ltd.)
Penguin Books India Pvt. Ltd., 11 Community Centre, Panchsheel Park,
New Delhi - 110 017, India
Penguin Group (NZ), 67 Apollo Drive, Rosedale, North Shore 0745,
Auckland, New Zealand (a division of Pearson New Zealand Ltd.)
Penguin Books (South Africa) (Pty.) Ltd., 24 Sturdee Avenue,
Rosebank, Johannesburg 2196, South Africa

Penguin Books Ltd., Registered Offices:
80 Strand, London WC2R 0RL, England

Published by Signet, an imprint of New American Library,
a division of Penguin Group (USA) Inc.

First Printing, August 1981
First Printing (Author Introduction), October 2007
10 9 8 7 6 5 4 3 2 1

For D.J.W. and General Lee

Few things are more illuminating than our own sense of darkness. . . .

—R. WAYNE WHITE

Introduction

In the winter of 1980, I received a surprising phone call from an editor at Signet Books—surprising because, as a Florida fishing guide, the only time New Yorkers called me was to charter my boat. And if any of my clients were editors, they were savvy enough not to admit it.

The editor said she'd read a story by me in *Outside Magazine* and was impressed. Did I have time to talk?

As a mediocre high school jock, my idols were writers, not ball players. I had a dream job as a light-tackle guide, yet I was still obsessed with my own dream of writing for a living. For years, before and after charters, I'd worked hard at the craft. Selling a story to *Outside*, one of the country's finest publications, was a huge break. I was about to finish a novel, but this was the first time New York had called.

Yes, I had time to talk.

The editor, whose name was Joanie, told me Signet

wanted to launch a paperback thriller series that featured a recurring he-man hero. "We want at least four writers on the project because we want to keep the books coming, publishing one right after the other, to create momentum."

Four writers producing books with the same character?

"Characters," Joanie corrected. "Once we get going, the cast will become standard."

Signet already had a template for the hero. He was a Vietnam vet turned Key West fishing guide, she said, talking as if the man existed. He was surfer-boy blond, and he'd been friends with Hemingway.

I am not a literary historian, but all my instincts told me the timetable seemed problematic. I said nothing.

"He has a shark scar," Joanie added, "and he's freakishly strong. Like a man who lifts weights all the time."

The guys I knew who lifted weights were also freakishly clumsy, so . . . maybe the hero, while visiting a local aquarium, tripped during feeding time?

My brain was already problem-solving.

"He lives in Key West," she said, "so, of course, he has to be an expert on the area. That's why I'm calling. You live in Key West, and I liked your magazine story a lot. It seems like a natural fit."

Actually, I fished out of Sanibel Island, on Florida's Gulf Coast, a six-hour drive from Sloppy Joe's, but this was no time for petty details.

"Have you ever been to Key West?" I asked the editor. "Great sunsets."

Editors, I have since learned, can also be cagey. Joanie didn't offer me the job. She had already settled on three of the four writers, she said, but if I was willing to submit a few sample chapters on speculation, she'd give me serious consideration.

Money? A contract? That stuff was "all standard," she told me, and could be discussed later.

"I'll warn you right now," she said, "there are a couple of other writers we're considering, so you need to get at least three chapters to me within a month. Then I'll let you know."

I hung up the phone, stunned by my good fortune. My first son, Lee, had been born only a few months earlier. My much adored wife, Debra, and I were desperate for money because the weather that winter had been miserable for fishing. But it was *perfect* for writing.

I went to my desk, determined not to let my young family down.

At Tarpon Bay Marina, where I was a guide, my friend Ralph Woodring owned a boat with *Dusky* painted in big blue letters on the side. My friend, Graeme Mellor, lived on a Morgan sailboat named *No Mas*.

Dusky MacMorgan was born.

Every winter, Clyde Beatty-Cole Bros. Circus came to town. Their trapeze artists, I realized, were not only freakishly strong, but they were also freakishly nimble.

Dusky gathered depth.

One of my best friends was the late Dr. Harold Westervelt, a gifted orthopedic surgeon. Dr. Westervelt became the Edison of Death, and he loved introducing himself that way to new patients. His son, David, became Westy O'Davis, and our spear-fishing pal, Billy, became Billy Mack.

Problems with my hero's shark scar and his devoted friendship with Hemingway were also solved.

Working around the clock, pounding away at my old black manual typewriter, I wrote *Key West Connection* in nine days. On a Monday morning, I waited for the post office to open to send it to New York.

Joanie sounded a little dazed when she telephoned on Friday. Was I willing to try a second book on spec?

Hell, yes.

God, I was beginning to *love* New York's can-do attitude.

The other three writers (if they ever existed) were fired, and I became the sole proprietor of Captain Dusky MacMorgan—although Signet owned the copyright and all other rights after I signed Joanie's "standard" contract. (This injustice was later made right by a willing and steadfast publisher and my brilliant agent.)

If Joanie (a fine editor) feels badly about that today, she shouldn't. I would've signed for less.

I wrote seven of what I would come to refer to as "duck and fuck" books because in alternating chapters Dusky would duck a few bullets, then spend much-deserved time alone with a heroine.

Seldom did a piece of paper go into my old typewriter that was ripped out and thrown away, and I suspect that's the way the books read. I don't know. I've never reread them. I do remember using obvious clichés, a form of self-loathing, as if to remind myself that I should be doing my *own* writing, not this job-of-work.

The book you are now holding, and the other six, constituted a training arena for a young writer who took seriously the discipline demanded by his craft and also the financial imperatives of being a young father.

For years, I apologized for these books. I no longer do.

—Randy Wayne White
Cartagena, Colombia

1

Less than ten minutes after the props of my thirty-four-foot sportfisherman, *Sniper*, almost cut the girl into fish-bait, the boat exploded.

Not my boat.

Some kind of commercial trawler. Hard to tell for sure. There wasn't much left of it.

It went up with a dazzling flash and rumble on the near horizon which turned the full-moon night to eerie day and exposed the mangrove jungle shoreline of the Ten Thousand Islands in a negative of stark whites and shadowed blacks. It was so unexpected that, for one crazy moment, I grabbed my head, thinking that I had been clubbed. But then, in the brightness of the explosion, I saw the burning four-foot wall of shock wave coming at us, and all we could do was hold fast and bow into it.

We were supposed to be on a vacation cruise.

A little rest and recreation for me and a wild Irish friend of mine, Westy O'Davis. I had met O'Davis down in Mariel Harbor, Cuba. Mariel was an ideal place for making quick friends and influencing deadly enemies. The Irishman had, in the period of less than twenty-four hours, become a close friend. He also happened to have saved my life. Twice.

And he wasn't about to let me forget it.

So he had come to visit me on my little house built on stilts out on the clearwater flats of Calda Bank near the pirate island of Key West, where I moor my charterboat, *Sniper.* For years it was a valued way of life—working as a fishing guide, going down every morning to the docks at Garrison Bight where my sign reads:

> *Captain Dusky MacMorgan*
> *Billfish, Dolphin, Sharks, Grouper*
> *Full days, Half days—inquire at Marina*

I didn't make much money as a fishing guide. But on the other side of the ledger, I had all the good clear fishing days a man could want, pretty nice tourist people to show a good time to, and best of all I was my own boss. Once I also had a fine wife and twin boys who were the best of both of us. But then the drug pirates got them, and I had nothing.

So I went back to doing what I did best—the

deadly trade I learned as a Navy SEAL. Revenge is not an ideal reason for living, but it's certainly one of the most compelling.

And I have lived fully since.

Especially in Mariel Harbor, Cuba.

So, after that ordeal, it seemed reasonable that O'Davis and I take a little time off. O'Davis, who works for that labor-union-ruled island called Great Britain, is a leprechaun giant with red beard, copper hair, and a Viking face which speaks with the amused black humor of the Irish poet. O'Davis had gone to Mariel from his island home in the Caymans, where his cover occupation includes leading scuba-diving tours and squiring around the pretty tourist ladies.

But he had had enough of government work and killing, and so had I, so we had spent that first week on my stilthouse drinking cold beer, battling good fish on light tackle, and telling tall tales. Then one night, while I sat with beer, a good book, and a fresh dip of Copenhagen, O'Davis began to go through my library of Florida charts. He unrolled them one by one, studying them, humming some strange tune as he did. I watched his broad face in the yellow light of the kerosene lamp.

"I want those all rolled back and catalogued the way I had them, O'Davis."

"Tum-da-dum-dum-dum . . . what?" And when I repeated it, he made a face of mock outrage.

"An' do ya think me some kind of slovenly child, Dusky MacMorgan, that ya be remindin' me to care for yer precious charts?"

"I do."

"Hah! An' now yer laughin' at me to boot!" He made as if to throw down the chart he was holding, then thought better of it. "So this is the thanks I get for savin' the life of the likes of you—and a big ugly brute you are, too. . . ."

"Oh God, O'Davis."

"I'll wager ya didna think me a slovenly child when meself, Westy O'Davis, clouted the Cuban guard who was about ta shoot ya."

"Do I have to listen to this again?"

"An' knocked the bloody Russian rifle from the other guard's hands."

"O'Davis?"

"Jest when he was about ta shoot ya, ya ugly little snit."

"O'Davis. Just tell me why you're looking at the charts. Okay?"

He stopped in midsentence, looked at me, and grinned. It was the kind of pleasant banter we had been enjoying all week; the kind the big Irishman reveled in. He rattled the chart meaningfully and said grandly, "Because, brother MacMorgan, tomorrow we're gettin' on that black-hulled power demon of yers and takin' a trip. All week long ya've been tellin' me that the only coastal wilderness left in Florida is the southwest coast, an' now that I've seen the Ten Thousand Islands on a chart, I want to see them in real life."

I shrugged, hiding my enthusiasm. Truth was, my stilthouse is awfully close quarters for two big men. And I, like the Irishman, was getting a little antsy. Besides, I loved the Ten Thousand Islands and the wilderness below it. On a map of Florida, it looks like the area below Naples and that concrete grotesquerie called Marco Island breaks into a massive jigsaw puzzle of windswept islands and sea. It's wild and deserted—a hundred miles of tidal rivers and mangrove islands and stretches of desolate beaches.

"Bugs will be bad," I said.

"Devil take the bugs."

"I have a friend who lives on one of the back-country islands. He's a hermit."

"The island with all the tarpon?"

I nodded. "But there'll be no women, O'Davis. Don't forget that. You're not going to be able to slip into Key West like you did last night and cat around."

He put on his special lecherous look and winked at me, a big bawdy wink. "And after last night, who needs the ladies, brother MacMorgan? I felt like a candle in a town full of moths, I did— so who needs 'em now?"

So that's how we happened to be cruising off White Horse Key on a full-moon night in June. It had taken us three very lazy days of fishing and diving to get across Florida Bay and idle our way along Cape Sable, past the mangrove giants of Shark River. We had spent the best of the twilight nosing around Indian Key Pass on the outgoing tide, taking five good snook on sweetened jigs— and releasing four. So now I steered from the main controls of the cabin, vectoring in on the distant flare of Coon Key Light with the vague idea of running Dismal Key Pass into the back country where the tarpon would be rolling in sheens of silver moonlight by the old houseboat across from Dismal Key.

Because of the bright moon, we ran without lights. The VHF was squelched off in favor of a Fort Myers radio station that fed a steady diet of classic old jazz throughout *Sniper*. O'Davis was up on the flybridge supposedly watching for crabpot buoys that could foul *Sniper*'s twin brass wheels— but he was actually gazing at the moon, drinking beer, and singing. It is the secret belief of most ethnic descendants that the little ethnic legends are full-blown truths, as if some mystic source seeds our brains with the talents of ancient birthright. With Italians it is cooking, with the French it is love, with the Swedes it is sailing, and with the Irish it is singing. I don't know about the Italians, French, and Swedes, but Westy O'Davis was seriously shortchanged in his atavistic talents. His Irish tenor sounded more like a water spaniel having difficulties with a bear. Even so, he still loved to sing— and that's really why he was up on the flybridge.

I was relaxed, listening to the strains of vintage Cole Porter waft across water and airwaves, studying the hulking shadow of mainland coast. *Sniper* was running a conservative twenty knots, and the silver expanse of sea spread out before us. It was a good night to sip at a cold beer and enjoy the nocturnal desolation only the sea and certain northern forests can offer, and I was caught up in the beauty of it all when the roaring voice of O'Davis snapped me out of my reverie.

"Back 'er, Dusky! Back 'er *now*, Yank!"

At sea you don't question a command like that—and back her I did, driving both gears into abrupt reverse, cringing with the strain I knew was being put on the transmission. There was a slight *clunk* against the fiberglass hull, then nothing. I switched the engines off, then went running back to the aft deck.

"What the hell did you see, you crazy—"

"There's someone out there, Yank!" He pointed anxiously to port. "Someone swimmin'—I swear it. Thought it was a bloody dog at first!"

And then I saw it too. A dark shadow on the silver veil of water. Someone clinging to something. Someone weak. Floundering. And disappearing rapidly astern as the momentum of *Sniper* carried us onward. In one long step, I was on the transom, then diving headlong into the night sea. I swam with head up, keeping a close eye on the dark shape in the distance. Behind me, I heard O'Davis start *Sniper* and turn to follow.

It was a person, all right. Someone hanging onto one of those cheap weekender life vests. The Coast Guard says the vests are fine for a pleasure craft. And they are—if said pleasure craft doesn't sink. I tried shouting. And got a low moan for an answer. So I made a quick forward approach, grabbed a dangling arm, pulled and took chin firmly in right hand, then switched to a cross-chest carry with my left.

And that's when I realized my victim was a woman. A well-formed woman. And almost naked.

O'Davis came up carefully behind us, reversed engines expertly, and rigged the boarding ladder. I slung her over my shoulder in a fireman's carry and pulled her up onto *Sniper*. He had a blanket ready, and I put her down back first onto the deck. The cabin lights were on, and you could see her clearly. She looked about twenty or twenty-one, though she could have been a few years older. Her blond hair, cut as short as a boy's, surrounded a fine angular face with a strong nose and full mouth. She was short: all breasts and shoulders with slender hips and thin legs. She wore brief jean shorts and that was all. No rings. No necklace. As surprised as I that she was naked, O'Davis quickly pulled the blanket up around her—an admirable show of character, because, as they say in the commercials, she was a very full-figured girl.

"Do ya know first aid, Yank?" We stood shoulder to shoulder staring at the girl in the blanket.

Sniper's engines burbled quietly in the moonlight, and somewhere a wading bird squawked.

"I do for drowning—but she wasn't drowning. She had a life vest. I think we may have clipped her with the hull when we went by."

O'Davis knelt and gently searched the fine blond hair with his meaty hand. "Aye. There's a lump here, sure enough." He looked up at me. "What in bloody hell do ya think she was doin' at midnight a quarter mile offshore in the Ten Thousand Islands?"

I shook my head. "Damned if I know. Maybe she was on a boat that went down. Or went for a swim and got caught by the tide. It happens."

The Irishman picked her up and carried her down into the forward vee-berth. She moaned softly, stretched her neck as if to yawn, then opened her eyes. The shock registered when she realized that she was on a strange boat, and both hands strained to pull the blanket tightly around her body. "Hey! Where am I? Who are you? What in the hell do you—"

"Shush . . . shush now, child," O'Davis said gently. He reached to pat her head, and she jerked violently away.

"Keep your goddamn hands off me!" She threw herself back on the bunk, twisting her head away.

I looked at the Irishman. "Like moths to a candle flame, huh?"

"Ah, she's young, Yank. Very young. But give 'er time and she'll be baskin' in me light."

"Well, we're not going to give her much time, because I'm calling the Coast Guard right now and have them send out a helicopter. A head injury is nothing to toy with—"

"No!" It was the girl, sitting up again, a wild look in her eyes. "No, don't call the Coast Guard. Please—"

I didn't have time to ask her why she didn't want me to notify the Coast Guard. Because that's when the sea turned to fire. And the mangroves a quarter mile away were caught in a stark white light—the same fiery light that showed me the shock wave rolling toward us.

That's when the boat—less than eight hundred yards away—suddenly exploded, lighting *Sniper* in its orange chromosphere, and catching a sudden slight smile on the face of the girl. . . .

2

It wasn't what you would have called a tidal wave.

Nothing deadly about it.

But the surge from the explosion was still big and weighty, and the breaker pounded *Sniper*; it sent my beer crashing in the galley, and threw the copy of *International-National Rules of the Road* I had been studying across the salon. Every five years I have to renew my Ocean Operator's License. First time around there were tests on International, Inland, Great Lakes, and Western Rivers, Rules of the Road, plus navigation, basic knots, basic diesel mechanics, and safety rules and regulations. After I had passed the three sections of the test, one at a time, they gave me a physical, fingerprinted me, swore me in, and I was an official fishing guide, duly licensed by the Coast Guard. Now, once every five years, I have to go to the testing center for a Rules of the Road "exercise"—which means an open-book test.

But I like to stay ahead of the game. You rarely, if ever, need some of the esoteric bits of information they ask you—like how often do you hear a five-second bell and a gong and need to know it signals a vessel over 350 feet at anchor in a fog? I've seen plenty of big vessels at anchor, but I've never ever heard them use the gong. But it pays to stay ahead of the game, as I said. And after five years, memory is faulty at best. So a month or so before it's time for me to renew my license, I get the new edition of *Rules of the Road* and hit the books, driving the bits and pieces of maritime law into my brain.

So anyway, it was one hell of an explosion. A big orange thermal flare that turned the wilderness darkness of the Ten Thousand Islands to fiery dawn.

Then a loud diesel *whoosh*, a wall of heat, and then the fire.

For the briefest moment, I saw the skeletal outline of the boat: some kind of shrimp trawler, maybe.

Then there was nothing but flames, three stories high, doing their eerie dance on the full-moon sea.

The fire—and that low wall of surge, was rolling at us and throwing flames, fuel on the surface burning like a storm wave from hell.

"Sweet Jesus, look at that bloody bugger!"

It was Westy. But I didn't have time for conversation. I ran to the controls and swung myself into the pilot chair. The wave was coming from sea- ward, where the ship had exploded, and we were between it and the mainland, pointing north. I hit both throttles and the twin 453 GMC diesels roared to action, bringing us around.

The wave was cresting, still aflame. I idled toward it, knowing what I wanted to do. The size of the wave was no problem. On one trip to the Dry Tortugas, *Sniper* had handled storm swells five times as big during one long-gone hurricane season.

But those monsters weren't burning.

I kept idling toward it, waiting for just the right moment. I didn't want any of that burning diesel washing over my decks. And just before it hit us, I popped both throttles full forward, jumping *Sniper* onto semi-plane, raising the bow and driving us safely through it. I heard glass clattering down in the galley, and I heard O'Davis swear.

I turned around. The forward thrust had knocked him ass-backward across the fighting deck.

"Ya might warn a fella, brother MacMorgan!" He had a ludicrous expression on his big red face, like a heavyweight caught by a surprise right hook thrown by a little kid.

"Didn't think a little swell like that would bother a heavy-water sailor like yourself, O'Davis."

He climbed nimbly to his feet and grabbed the

brace bar beside the pilot chair. "Never been no finer blue-water sailor than meself, ya little snit— it's this bloody speedboat o' yers I'm not used to. Stinkin', smoky things they are, too. . . ."

"Westy?"

"Belchin' their nasty fumes across God's blue waters, chokin' the little birds 'n beasties."

"Hey!"

"An' ya needn't yell at me either!" He had a look of mock outrage on his face, but underneath it he was smiling. And before I could even ask, he told me what I wanted to know. He said, "The child is still below, doin' jest fine, I'm thinkin'. Took that little bit of a flashlight o' yers and checked her pupils. Still wouldn't hurt ta get her to a doctor, but her eyes looked fine—pretty eyes they are, too."

"You're a dirty old man, O'Davis."

"Hah! And I admit it, I do!"

Behind us, the enormous swell had crashed onto the moonswept beach of White Horse Key, its flames spent. Ahead of us, the remains of the mystery boat still burned. I powered *Sniper* toward it, full-bore. I had the big 500,000-candlepower deck light on, and the Irishman swept it back and forth before us without my having to ask. That's what makes a good boatmate—they think for themselves, and do what should be done without having to be told.

"So did she say anything before you came up?"

He shook his head. "Nary a word. Jest kept tellin' me that she wasn't hurt. Asked her how she happened ta be takin' a swim out here in th' middle o' nowhere, an' she didn't even have the courtesy ta answer."

"Seems a tad suspicious to me—we find her, then a boat explodes."

"If ya have a suspicious mind, it does."

"I do."

He looked at me, the grin gone in the white haze of moon and the red glow of the control panel. "An' I do too, Yank. But let's not be jumpin' ta conclusions. Poor lass is in shock, naturally. Mebbe someone out there kin tell us more about it."

He pointed to where the center of flames flickered before us. Maybe there were survivors. But I doubted it. It was one hell of an explosion. But maybe I *was* jumping to conclusions. Explosions aren't all that uncommon around boats. Fuel fumes build up in a gas-engine compartment, and someone tries to start the engines without hitting the ventilator switch first, and *boom.* You read about them all the time in the newspapers: the Power Squadron types who learn their seamanship from magazines, expecting a boat to be as easy and as safe to operate as their Cadillacs. All it takes is one simple mistake to send them back north in a closed casket with a one-way ticket to some less than heavenly place, where all the dead

weekend seamen must sit around and bore each
other to tears with their cocktail-party stories of
their high-seas exploits.

So maybe it was all just an accident. And a
coincidence.

Maybe. . . .

I skirted the aftermath of fire so that I was up-
wind of it, then I headed toward it at dead slow,
letting O'Davis work the light.

He swept it back and forth on the water, sin-
gling out bits and pieces of debris. Chunks of
deck. A commercial lifejacket. Two red embers of
eyes, and the oil-slick body of a rat swimming
toward shore.

"Hey, do ya see that?"

I did. A white life ring rolling in the weak sea.

While O'Davis got the boathook, I cut above it,
pulled the throttles back into idle, and drifted
down on the ring. It was a bright white corona in
the glare of my spotlight, the name on it in bold
red letters: *Blind Luck.*

On this night, someone's luck had run out. And
there were some very, very dead people around.

When the Irishman had the life ring aboard, I
switched on the VHF and contacted the Everglades National Park Service on my third call. The
officer seemed suspicious, and I didn't blame him.
Reporting a false emergency is one of the standard
drugrunner ploys. They call the Coast Guard and
give fake coordinates to disasters which have

never occurred. Then, with the Coasties busy searching for imaginary boats in contrived distress, the drugrunners have clear sailing to load and deliver their contraband.

Finally, when I repeated the name of my vessel for the fourth time, the officer seemed convinced, and he said he'd contact Key West Coast Guard, have them send up a jet copter.

"You said you weren't gonna call, damn it!"

It was the girl. She had come up from below. She wore one of the Irishman's huge cotton plaid shirts. It fit her like a sack. She held the ragged lifejacket against the lift of large breasts—obvious even in that shirt and in the flicker of fire and soft haze of moonlight. Her short blond hair had dried, like white spun glass, and her child's face pouted.

"You said I wasn't going to call—I didn't."

"You're a lying son of a—"

"Now, now, child." O'Davis came up behind her and put his hand on her shoulder, comforting her. She recoiled momentarily then let his big hand stay. "This big ugly brute kin be snappish at times, but ya have ta understand he's jest doin' his dooty. He's required by law—"

"I don't give a shit!"

She had a low alto voice, incongruous with the girlish face and baby-fat weight of breasts. It was a gravelly whiskey voice, straight from Bacall—and just as brash.

"An' I kin understand that—but lass, you've

had a strenuous night. Come with meself below
and I'll give ye a tech o' fine Irish whiskey ta
make ya feel better."

O'Davis guided her down into the main cabin,
gently mediating her protestations.

I checked my watch. The big luminescent numerals of the Rolex said it was nearly midnight.
The full moon was heading westward, following
the long-gone sun.

I swept *Sniper* back and forth above the flames,
searching. More debris: chunks of wood, mangled
Tupperware, clots of clothing, and a weak haze of
dust that made me sneeze. That's what's left when
a boat goes down: dust and oil on the empty sea.
Westy came back above.

"How's she doing?"

"Better, Yank. Better. Took all me charm ta settle her—and that's sayin' something. Seems on the
edge of hysterics, she does."

"Still didn't say anything?"

"Give 'er time, brother MacMorgan. She will,
she will."

The Irishman climbed up to the flybridge to
handle the spotlight and act as lookout. I powered
Sniper abeam the flames, riding the weak roll of
night sea downwind. There was more debris now;
odd shapes in the harsh glare of light.

"What's that stuff?"

"Bloody garbage bags. Hundreds of 'em, mate!"

It didn't take long to dawn on me. Not many
commercial trawler boats carry garbage bags. Call

it laziness or call it expedience, but most of them just dump their junk into the sea. You'd think that people who make their living on and from the ocean would treat it with more grace, but they don't. The idea of the kindly old commercial fisherman filled with reverence for the sea is largely a myth. You see that character in Walt Disney movies but rarely anyplace else. Sixty percent of the commercial crewmen fish because they aren't smart enough to do anything else—not that you can be stupid and be a consistently good fisherman. You can't. And many of them aren't. Gradually, they come to hate their stinking, jury-rigged boats and the bad hours, the rough work, and the low wages—and contempt for the sea which holds them is the natural progression in the unfortunate disorder of their lives. And they take their hatred out on the sea by treating it as if they own it—when, in fact, it owns them. They toss their cans and bottles overboard, and try to punish it with their bilge oil gunk and their engine poisons, and in the end, as the fish head ever deeper and disappear, they just end up punishing themselves.

So I doubted if those garbage bags held garbage.

"Let's have a look, Westy."

"Jest thinkin' that meself, Yank."

I brought *Sniper* down on one of the big floating bags, reversed her, and shut her down. In the new silence, my twin diesels *tick-click-ticked* with heat and the dying sea fire *whooshed* with every gust of freshening night breeze. *Sniper* rolled gently, and rust-colored cirrus clouds scudded beneath the high bright moon.

As the Irishman scampered his bulk down to the aft deck, I grabbed the long boathook and pulled at one of the garbage bags.

"Watch ya doona strain yerself there, Yank."

"Well, if you'd help instead of standing there grinning it would be a hell of a lot easier."

"Jest didna want ta get in yer way."

O'Davis climbed down in the diving platform when I had the bag near the boat. He grabbed it in two huge arms, lifted, and swung it aboard with an ease that made me feel like a weakling. O'Davis is one of the strongest men I have ever met, no doubt about that. He stands right at six feet, weighs about as much as me, and looks like one of those Olympic-class two-hundred-pounders, all chest and forearms. He ripped the bag open and pulled out a handful of something that looked like water-soaked hay. He sniffed it experimentally.

"Is it?"

"Well now, I'm no expert, brother MacMorgan, but I'd say the poor lads on this boat were either hauling horse fodder ta Kentucky—or tryin' ta get rich dealin' in the evil herb."

"Horse fodder, huh? Why is it all you Irishmen consider yourselves poets?"

He winked at me. " 'Cause we are, mate. We are."

"Just like you can all sing tenor."

"Ah, I kin, I kin. A lovely voice I have, don't you think?"

I brushed at my chin, trying not to chuckle. Funny guy, Westy O'Davis.

Unless things got rough.

And then I was just happy as hell to have him on my side.

"Let's check out some more of those bags. The Coasties should be getting here pretty soon."

"An' I thought we were on vacation, brother MacMorgan."

"Like I said—I'm nosy."

"Nosy and suspicious, eh?"

"Right."

We found the cocaine in a half-dozen smaller garbage bags. It had been triple-wrapped in those modern magic-lock sandwich bags, then again in burlap. Each of the smaller bags weighed about a pound. There were ten to a garbage bag—sixty of them in all. And probably a hell of a lot more out there in the night sea. Or burned and ruined. It was a gold mine. No, better than a gold mine. While O'Davis went through the bags, I did some mental figuring. Straight from Colombia, the cocaine was probably seventy-five to ninety percent pure, uncut stuff. Everyone who handled it would cut it a little more. They use quinine or some sort of powdered laxative, because cocaine dries out the system. By the time it gets to the street it's only one to fifteen percent pure. If someone—even a regular user— took a hit of this uncut stuff, or a "hot shot," it would either kill them or they wouldn't crap for a week. Which is why they cut it with a laxative. Street value of the cut stuff was what? One to two thousand dollars per ounce, depending on the quality. The uncut cocaine in these bags would go wholesale—but even so, we had fished out two to four million dollars' worth. And that wasn't even counting the grass, which wholesales for about a hundred to two hundred bucks a pound. And it hits the streets at over twenty dollars an ounce.

So someone had planned on getting very, very damn rich.

It sounds so simple. Buy one of those big long-distance trawlers. Visit South America, party for a week, pick up one load—maybe two—and you're immediately wealthy enough to retire.

But something had gone wrong on the vessel *Blind Luck.*

Approaching the mainland of Florida's Ten Thousand Islands, her crew had probably been worried only about the feds and the Coast Guard—knowing full well that fewer than ten percent of the drugrunners are ever caught, and only about two percent of those ever see the inside of a prison after their day in court.

But it wasn't the Coasties or the feds they had to worry about.

It was an explosion. One hell of an explosion that had scattered their pieces among the fish and their dream-making drug gold.

Accidental?

Maybe.

Or maybe some organized competition had taken them out. The big boys will tolerate the amateur only so long. They don't mind letting them make small scores. But when certain small fry start getting greedy, the organized-crime boys can come down hard. Hard and deadly. The boats the amateurs use are normally found shot up, blood-stained, and empty.

Or never found at all.

The pros are utterly ruthless—I know that all too well. I'm no paragon of virtue, but anyone who would get rich by slowly destroying the minds—and the lives—of others . . . well, a quick death is too good for them.

So I wasn't exactly filled with grief for the victims on the late *Blind Luck*.

I checked my Rolex again. The Coast Guard would be arriving soon. I had given them loran coordinates, so they wouldn't have any trouble finding us.

"O'Davis."

"Aye?"

"Let's start tossing the drugs back in. I don't want the Coasties to get any wrong ideas about us."

And that's when I heard it. We both heard it. We stopped, heads turned, straining to listen: a low, agonized groan in the darkness.

The Irishman jumped for the light. "Someone's out there, mate!"

Sound travels well over water, but direction is distorted. So it took us a while to find him among the rest of the debris. But finally, O'Davis brought the light to bear on him: a man clinging to a partially submerged bale of marijuana, face blackened, hair oil-soaked, horribly burned.

3

He was a kid, really.

Late teens, early twenties—stocky, with muscle already turning to fat. He looked like he might once have played guard for some second-rate high school football team before he became a part of the drug culture. He had dark hair down to his shoulders, and one lone earring, and the side of his face that wasn't burned was covered with the fuzz of a beard that just wouldn't grow.

I approached him from downwind, cutting the wheel at the last moment so that we would take him over the dive platform. The Irishman lifted him like a kid lifting a sick kitten. He swung him around and put him gently on the deck. I had a wool Navy-issue blanket waiting. The wind gusted, rolling *Sniper* and thrusting the acrid odor of death at my face. I cringed. Couldn't help it. I had seen and smelled too much of it back in Nam.

It's an odor you never forget. The impact stays with you, even if you can't recall the finely etched details of the horror. And now it slapped me in the face—the smell of charred flesh, skin burst from flame, hair singed to powder, and, along with it, an odd odor of dryness—like the scent of death itself.

But I felt no compassion for the drugrunners who had been aboard *Blind Luck.*

These lowlifes, many of whom thought of themselves as part of the romantic tradition of pirates and great seafarers—the moonrakers, the smugglers, the rumrunners—were actually nothing more than human leeches. They sold wholesale dreams. They dealt in escape and, in the process, bartered souls for cold cash.

No, I was damn short on compassion for the likes of organized drug dealers. One of their kind had killed my wife, my two young sons, and my best friend. I knew just how ruthless they were. And at times, when the blind rage of memory was upon me, I knew that a quick death was too good for them.

And yet, looking down on the charred distortion of this thing which had once been a healthy human being, I felt a rush of empathy. Poor bastard. Hell of a way to go. Back in Nam, that was my great fear—death by fire.

And it still is.

Westy O'Davis bent over the kid, checking his eyes and pulse carefully, turning his big Irish face toward me in the periphery of the moon and white deck lights. He lifted an eyebrow, meaning something. He said, " 'Tis amazin', it is. Kid's still alive, Yank. Poor heart's jest poundin' away like nothin' ever happened." He looked skyward momentarily as if above us, in the silver haze of moon and cold swirl of stars, he expected to see . . . what?

Something. Just something. Something other than the stark beauty of night and infinite universe. I knew the urge; that instinctive thrust of desire to see just what the hell is up there looking out for all the wronged and beaten and burned.

"Amazin'," Westy said again, his voice trailing off.

"What's amazing?"

It was the girl again. In a sweeping glance, she took in the drugs sacked and piled on *Sniper's* aft deck, and this new human cargo, too.

"My God," she said, hand to her mouth, horrified. She took an involuntary step backward, then forced herself to draw closer. The kid was not a very pretty sight, no doubt about that. He had been wearing a blue windbreaker, or something plastic, anyway, and it had melted onto the scorched skin; the jeans he had worn were now smudges of ash.

"Is he . . . is he . . ."

"No, lass," the Irishman said softly. He still had his big hands pressed to the kid's wrist, keeping close tabs on the pulse. "No, he's not dead."

The girl hustled down beside us now, bending

over him as we settled into that silence which is
the equivalent of a deathwatch. No matter how
often I see it, that final moment between breath
and death still fills me with mild surprise. For all
the thought we give it, for all the writing which
has been done about it, death is such a simple
thing. One moment there is a heartbeat. The next
moment there is nothing. And the body's inhabi-
tant, with its thought and fear and laughter, seems
to just disappear, like a parachutist abandoning a
disabled plane or a tourist checking out of a hotel.

But this kid wasn't about to give up residency
yet.

The girl put her hands on my shoulders and
shoved me roughly away. A lot of strength in
those arms for such a little girl. "Dammit," she
said, "we've got to do something! You—" She
shoved at me again. "You get some more blankets.
He's in shock. We've got to get his feet up. The
shock will kill him faster than the burns!"

And as quickly as that, she was in charge. She
made O'Davis pick up the burned drugrunner and
carry him below. She still wore his baggy plaid
shirt, short blond hair plastered to her head like
Joan of Arc, yammering at the big Irishman like
a poodle bossing a bear. He laid him forward, on
the big vee-berth. With two single men staying
aboard *Sniper*, you would have expected her to be
sloppy down below. But when it came to boats,
Westy O'Davis was as fussy about neatness as I.
Like fastidious old ladies, we had cleaned and

straightened after ourselves, day in, day out, the way it should be done aboard any vessel. So there was no hasty sweeping away of dirty clothes and personal gear when the big Irishman put the kid down. Just the soaking life preserver the girl had clung to hanging on the foul-water rail along the extra bunk, the musty odor of bedding and the fiberglass and diesel reek of *Sniper* in the single overhead cabin light.

The girl had been transformed. Before, she was just some foulmouthed stranger who had suffered some unknown accident. One of the distant ones; uncommunicative, aloof—displaying the kind of sensuous indifference shown by a certain brand of teenager toward adults.

But now she was trying to save this burned kid. And she worked with the professional intensity of a trained medic.

And by the look on O'Davis's face, I could tell that he was as surprised as I.

"We got to get his feet up." She glanced quickly around the cabin and saw what she needed. She pushed the Irishman, and he propped up the kid's feet with the two pillows she had indicated, while she covered him with my Navy-issue blanket. Then she turned on me. "And you—you get a big tub or something. A bucket, maybe."

"Yeah?"

"And fill it with salt water. Then put all the ice you can find in it. Well move, damn it!"

So I moved. I'm not one of those lucky people

who are smart or energetic enough to develop expertise in a broad assortment of fields. I'm the master of a few, mediocre at most, a complete zero at the rest. But I knew enough about first aid to understand what the girl had in mind. And she was right. This kid had been burned so badly he hadn't even blistered much. Third-degree burns. Both epidermis and dermis destroyed, with damage extending deep into the charred flesh. If he was to live, he needed someone like this girl to take control. He lay there in the stink of his own injuries. The long brown hair was surprisingly intact. The earring he wore glistened in the light. And the rest of him lay beneath the blanket, breath fluttering, dying.

I got the biggest container I could find—a five-gallon pickle bucket I used for chum. I swung down on the teak boarding platform, rinsed it quickly, and loaded it with salt water. I noticed absently that we still drifted on the moonlit sea. I'd have to drop the hook soon. The soft heave of sea and tide were pushing us toward the darkness of the Ten Thousand Islands. The Coon Key marker flashed briefly in the far distance. Say what you want about Florida, but there is still wilderness, still places where wildlife and fish outnumber the billboards and condominiums. And short of the Everglades or the gulf stream, this was the biggest wilderness of them all.

I carried the water below. The girl knelt beside the charred young man. She glanced at me briefly as I got ice from my little refrigerator and transferred it to the bucket.

"You'll need some towels, right?"

"Right," she said. "And quick."

I knew what she was doing. If the kid regained consciousness, the pain would be unbearable. Unless he was covered with cold compresses. Or submerged in cold water. And since it was June and the water was warm, she was going to sponge him with iced water.

I placed the bucket beside her and got a half-dozen cotton towels from the head.

She knew what she was doing, all right. One by one, she placed the towels in succession over the kid. And when the last one was in place, she soaked, wrung out, and replaced the first. It was in my mind that she should have cut the remnants of his pants and jacket away and put the towels in closer contact with his skin. But then I realized that I was wrong. Pull his clothes off and the skin would probably come with it. She worked with professional concentration. She was no longer the trembling survivor I had pulled from the midnight sea. Nothing like work to refocus the brain and steady the nerves. And this woman was doing work she seemed to know well.

O'Davis and I exchanged looks. He lifted his eyebrows, as impressed as I.

He said, "You have the fine steady hand of a nurse, me dear."

She turned briefly. "I should. That's what I am.

What I was. . . ." She stopped, minor irritation crossing her face at having her guard pulled down so easily. O'Davis was a master at that. And she immediately turned her concentration back to her patient. She didn't want to talk. That was becoming increasingly clear. But why? What was she hiding? Maybe it was obvious. Maybe she had been a part of the drug boat, the *Blind Luck.* But how in the hell had she happened to go overboard before the explosion? Unless . . . unless she had set it?

Jumping to conclusions again. It happens. You see it in people all the time. Something in their life goes sour, and they begin to look upon the world with sour eyes. Every stranger becomes a threat. And every threat breeds suspicion, and a meanness that is nothing more than a reflection of the viewer.

And now I was seeing that suspicion, that meanness, in myself.

Because my world had gone sour.

And it would never ever be the same again.

I put my hand on the girl's shoulder. "You're doing a fine job," I said. "Anything more I can get for you?"

She looked up, surprised at the absence of the antagonism that had already built up between us. Her bright-green eyes shone in the cabin light, and her face was tan from long days in the Florida sun. It wasn't the carefully nurtured Palm Beach tan, either. No oily softness of creams and lotions.

There was only the softness of her youth, and a few sun-track lines about mouth and eyes.

She shook her head. "No. You said the Coast Guard was coming, right?"

I nodded.

"Helicopter?"

"They said they'd send one."

She wrung out another towel and folded it lightly over the kid's face. He groaned heavily, stirred, then lay still. "Then they'll be able to fly him right to a hospital. And they'll probably be carrying some morphine along for the shock. That's what he needs now. So no, there's nothing more you can do."

Westy stood up as if to leave, looked at the girl, who still bent attentively over the kid, then gave me a meaningful nod. I interpreted it correctly. He wanted to be alone with her. And he was right. O'Davis had the charm to get her story out of her. I didn't. It was as simple as that. So I went topside. Nice night. High bright stars and tropical moon. Good night for jumping tarpon on light tackle off Dismal Key. Or for beer and songs and old stories. Or for love. But not a fit night for exploding boats and charred bodies and mysterious young women.

But that's the way it happens. Like in the song: *When you least expect it . . .*

I checked the green glow of my Rolex Submariner.

A little after midnight.

And just as I was thinking that the Coast Guard deskman had jotted down our loran coordinates incorrectly, the big Coastie jet copter came zeroing in on us, searchlight sweeping the water with the intensity of a noonday sun. I swung *Sniper*'s deck light around and snapped off the correct dots and dashes: SOS.

It was one of the Coast Guard's big choppers. An H3 twin turbine. Out of Clearwater, probably, and temporarily based at Key West. The pilot brought her hovering over us, red and green running lights popping through the propeller swirl like some craft from another planet. Then he set her down sweetly in a deafening roar of wind and water. And when she had settled down upon her pontoons, he throttled down into idle—which was only slightly less deafening. But he didn't switch her off. And I didn't blame him. The Coasties have to be careful. They work in the middle of a lot of ocean and emptiness, and they never know for sure what they're dropping in on. So he kept the blades whirling and chose to talk to me first over their PA system:

"This is Petty Officer Barton of the United States Coast Guard speaking. Would you please identify yourself and your vessel and tell me the nature of your distress."

The clear, surprisingly youthful voice seemed to come from the bowels of the big chopper.

I switched my VHF to PA, picked up the mike, identified myself, and then responded, "Mr. Barton, about thirty minutes ago another vessel—an unidentified vessel—exploded. We've picked up one survivor. He's critically injured. There may be other survivors around. I don't know. But this guy needs some immediate medical attention. Request permission to transfer him to your chopper for transport."

Except for the high turbine roar of the chopper, there was a long silence. I could imagine what was going on within. The pilot would be radioing Key West or Clearwater for instructions. The chopper would be working in concert with a Coast Guard vessel probably heading for us at that very moment. Should they wait and assist? Or should they take the injured man aboard and head for the nearest hospital?—Naples, probably.

It was just a short formality. There was no doubt in my mind—or theirs either—what they would do. A lot of private boaters don't like the Coast Guard. They look upon it as troublesome with all its rules and regulations. Until they're in distress, that is. But when the going gets tough on the water, there's no one I'd rather have around than a watch of well-trained Coasties. In a month of active duty, they get more experience in heavy-water situations than most boaters get in a lifetime. For my money, the Coast Guard is the one bright spot in an otherwise bureaucratic Department of Transportation.

"Permission to transfer granted, Captain Mac-Morgan. Do you have a launch?"

"Yeah, but I think it would be faster if I brought my cruiser in bow-first."

"Negative. That's a negative. Please transfer by launch. We'll be waiting to assist."

Suspicious. Ever suspicious. But, they had their craft to worry about. They didn't know if I was an inept helmsman or not. So I didn't argue.

I didn't have to call O'Davis. He had heard everything. He brought the kid up wrapped in a blanket. The girl followed attentively alongside, still changing the cold towels. As always, I had my little thirteen-foot Boston Whaler tethered astern. A great little go-anywhere, take-any-sea boat, the Whaler. I had figured it would be a perfect fishing skiff on our little vacation in the Ten Thousand Islands. There's a lot of shoal water, and besides, it's easy to cast from.

I had never planned to use it as a transport vessel.

I climbed down on the boarding platform and hauled the Whaler in hand over hand, then snubbed her off short. O'Davis leaned over and handed me the kid. A lot of weight; I had to fight for balance. Somewhere between 170 and 180 pounds.

"Hurry up and get in the Whaler before I drop him, O'Davis."

"Are ya gettin' so old, brother MacMorgan, that ya canna hold a little bit of a thing like him? Hah!" He stepped over into the skiff nimbly, and

I handed him the injured drugrunner, straining to make it look effortless.

"Someday, O'Davis, I'll show you just what this old man can do. But now let's just concentrate on getting this kid to the chopper."

"Fine idea, fine idea, Yank."

The girl stayed aboard *Sniper*, watching us anxiously. I punched the combination key and choke, turned the switch, and the Whaler's fifty-horse outboard fired to life. The big Irishman cast off the lines. As we pulled away from *Sniper*'s stern, I leaned over and spoke in O'Davis's ear.

"Did you get anything out of her?"

"Ya wouldn't be doubtin' me charm now, would ye, Yank?"

"Can't you be serious even for a minute, O'Davis?"

He grew suddenly sober. "Aye, I kin. An' the little lady has had a tough time of it, she has. Don't have time ta tell ya the whole story now, Dusky, but just take me word that the lass has good reason for not wantin' ta get involved with the authorities."

"Was she with them—the drugrunners?"

"Aye—but not by choice, Yank. Stole 'er off the beach yesterday, they did. Used 'er as a play toy. Broke down when she told me. Doesn't want anyone ta find out." I felt his dark eyes level on me. "So I promised her, Dusky. Give her me word for both of us."

I slapped him on the knee. "If you're convinced, it's good enough for me, O'Davis. I'm not about to break one of your promises."

The Coast Guard crew had the big door amidships wide open to our approach. I dropped the Whaler down off plane as we neared, and the huge spotlight caught me full in the face momentarily, then swept away. They wanted some visual verification that we were, indeed, bringing an injured man with us. I cut the wheel and brought the little skiff in portside-to, then cut the engine while O'Davis handed them a line. The coxswain, Petty Officer Barton, was there to meet us. He reached down and shook hands while his men transferred the burned drugrunner.

"We've got a Coast Guard patrol vessel in the area, Captain MacMorgan," he yelled over the turbine whir of the jet copter.

He leaned out from the doorway, right hand clinging to an overhead brace. He wore the plain Coast Guard duty uniform and a dark-blue baseball cap with the initials CG in white. He was slightly built, medium height, with a full black beard that seemed incongruous with his youth. Although his manner was businesslike, it was edged with a natural friendliness.

"How soon before they get here?"

He made a nodding motion with his head. "You can see their running lights now. It's the cruiser *Royal Palm*. Chief Spears is in charge. Good man. You can give your report to him—"

The young officer stopped abruptly. Three men had been kneeling over the burned drugrunner, working on him. One had stood up suddenly and tapped Petty Officer Barton on the shoulder. They exchanged whispers solemnly.

"Is there some problem, Mr. Barton?"

The young officer nodded shortly. The friendliness was gone now, replaced by a professional frankness.

"Afraid so, Captain MacMorgan. It looks as if we'll be able to stay and assist the *Royal Palm* after all."

"But what about the kid?"

"He's dead, Captain MacMorgan. Already was when you brought him aboard. . . ."

4

At first, I thought they were joking when Chief Spears of the Coast Guard vessel *Royal Palm* arrested us and rattled off our rights.

I even nudged O'Davis and smiled.

He didn't smile back, though.

And that's when I knew that if it was a joke, no one else was laughing.

So the kid was dead. He and how many others? No way of knowing—not until dawn, anyway, when the morning sea started throwing corpses onto the deserted beaches of White Horse Key and Gullivan Key and Panther Key and the rest.

A lot of people have died in the wilderness of the Ten Thousand Islands. First when the Spaniards came and made unsuccessful war on the Calusa and Tequesta Indians, then when the Seminoles made their last desperate stands, and later in the late 1800s and early 1900s when runaway outlaws made that desolate tract of sea and islands their hideouts. And now it was the drug-runners, who would undoubtedly bring the number into the thousands.

When Petty Officer Barton suggested we return to *Sniper* and stand by, I kicked the little Whaler into gear and, in a couple of minutes, had her made fast again at the stern of my sportfisherman. The girl was in the galley, plaid shirt hanging down to her knees, making coffee. I noticed she had moved her ragged lifejacket to a hook above the little alcohol stove to dry. She made a brushing motion at her close-cropped blond hair when we came in and took a quick look out the little port.

"The helicopter hasn't left. Why haven't they taken off?"

I took three stoneware mugs from the galley locker and began to pour. The coffee was thin; tea-colored. Not strong enough for me, but I sipped at it anyway. "They're standing by to assist the Coast Guard cruiser. I checked the radar. It's not far off."

"But what about the man who was burned? If they don't get him to a hospital . . ."

"It's too late." I hesitated momentarily, realizing that I didn't even know this girl's name. "He's dead."

I watched the slow intake of breath, heavy breasts rising beneath the shirt. She looked honestly distressed. "Oh," she said simply.

"You did your best."

"What? Hmm . . ." She carried her coffee to the little galley booth and sat down heavily. She traced the lip of her coffee mug with an index finger absently. There was a strange, perplexed look on her face. It had been a tough night for us all. But for her it had been worse—a tough two, maybe three days. And now this final strain; the irony of having to nurse one of her captors, and then having that captor die.

She sat at the booth, sipped at her coffee, and suddenly shuddered. She wiped her face with a shaky hand. "Goddamn it," she said. "Goddamn it to hell. . . ." She turned and looked at me. The little overhead galley light left half of her young angular face in shadow. The light, plus her low, whiskey voice, made her seem older. "Where's your friend; the Irishman?"

"He's topside, setting an anchor."

"I told him . . . told him what happened. . . ." And then the tears came; a long sweeping veil of anguish. Her hands went automatically to her face, covering her eyes, and her elbow knocked over the mug of coffee, burning her.

"Shit!"

And then more tears, more anguish; uncontrollable sobs.

I grabbed a towel, blotted the coffee off the table. I hesitated, then dabbed at her leg. She recoiled momentarily, then leaned against me, burying her face in my shoulder.

"Goddamn it, I tried to save him—but I . . . I

wanted him to die. I really did. The son of a bitch . . . the stinking bastard . . .''

So what do you do when a strange woman cries on your shoulder? You make comforting noises and pat the warm back noncommittally, and you rock her gently and try to relieve some of the hurt by caring. When some of the logjam of hatred and profanity had been purged, I brushed her short hair back from her face, and then pulled a near-full flagon of peach brandy from the liquor locker. A friend of mine in Athens, Georgia, makes a new batch at the end of every peach harvest. He ages it in old oak casks that his father and his grandfather used before him, and every summer when he comes to Key West to fish for tarpon, he brings me a quart of that rare golden drink. I twisted the cork out and poured a healthy dollop into the mug, added coffee, and handed it to her. She picked it up and sniffed it.

"Drink it down," I said. "It'll make you feel better."

"I doubt that."

"Give it a try. It can't hurt."

She took a sip, then another, and began to say something. But she was interrupted by the sound of a boat coming.

"Coast Guard coming along starboard side, brother MacMorgan!"

O'Davis had his big Viking face poked through the main hatchway.

"Be right up."

She was a big steel displacement cruiser, probably sixty feet long. Lights glowed through the lower ports—where the midnight watch was probably drinking coffee, waking up, standing by. The superstructure of the *Royal Palm* was also lighted. Another watch stood in their bulky lifejackets and hard hats, ready to lower a launch.

A voice came over the PA system; an older voice, even more businesslike. "This is Chief Petty Officer Spears of the United States Coast Guard speaking. Please prepare to be boarded."

It was not a request. The Coast Guard doesn't have to ask. If they want to board, they board. Simple as that.

I left the girl with her laced coffee and made my way to *Sniper*'s aft deck, where Westy stood watching the big Coast Guard vessel reverse engines and drop anchor. He had hands on hips, head down.

"I fear we've forgotten somethin', Yank."

"And what could that be, Westy?"

He kicked at something with his foot, and I saw what he meant. The bale of marijuana still lay on the deck, black garbage bag pulled back. The bags of cocaine surrounded it.

"All we have to do is tell them the truth. Don't worry about it," I said.

He raised his eyebrows, his bearded countenance showing a wry dark humor.

"No offense, brother MacMorgan, but I'm a-thinkin' the only person aboard this stinkpot o' yours with an honest face is th' little lady below. Handsome as I am, folks tend to put their hands on their wallets when I come a-roamin'. And you, me friend—big and blond as ya are, you'll never pass as a choirboy."

"You worry too much, O'Davis."

"Hah! Never had much ta worry about till I met you, Yank!" He laughed loudly, his barrel chest heaving. "Come up here for a bit of a holiday, an' next thing I know we've got half the Coast Guard surroundin' us, a load o' drugs aboard, one dead man to our credit, and a half-drowned minor below—and you say I worry too much! Hah!"

He went on laughing to himself, switching from laughter to some strange Irish tune, tapping his foot and muttering. "Tum-de-dum-de-dum . . . worry too much, he says, the big ugly brute!"

There were six men in the launch. It was a true inboard, built like the old whaling boats with pointed bow and stern, complete with tiller. They brought her alongside professionally, and Chief Spears jumped aboard along with two other men before their skiff was even tied off. They were all armed. His two men carried automatic weapons, M-16s. The chief was a broad-shouldered, broad-necked guy with a stub of cigar in his mouth, and he carried a .45 service automatic on his hip, holster unsnapped. He was a couple of inches under six feet, maybe thirty-five or thirty-six years old, and weighed close to two-hundred pounds—hard to tell with the bulky life vest covering his frame.

Like the rest of his men he wore a short-sleeved duty shirt, and his biceps bulged from beneath. But bulky as he was, the big Irishman and I dwarfed him. I saw his eyes harden at the impact of our size. He looked at me first, and then at O'Davis.

"Which of you is the master of this vessel?"

Westy motioned with his head. "The ugly one, sar."

Spears almost grinned. But then his eyes caught what was lying behind us on the deck. He nodded to his men. They moved backward toward the cache of drugs, faces trained on us, weapons ready.

"Bale of grass and a shitpot full of coke, Chief," one of his men said.

Spears looked at me. He had tough dark eyes. I could almost see his mind working. A drug boat explodes and we just happen to be in the area. What were we? A pickup boat? Or maybe just some muscle hired by the Miami mob to knock off one more group of amateurs.

Whatever he thought, Chief Spears wasn't taking any chances.

"MacMorgan, is it?"

"That's right, Chief."

"I suppose you can explain that pile of drugs there?"

I nodded. "Right again."

He touched my elbow, right hand on the grip of his automatic. "Well, Captain MacMorgan, before you get into detailed explaining, do you mind if I accompany you below and have a look at your papers?"

It sounded like a request. But it wasn't.

I keep my ship's papers in a waterproof ammo box I rescued from Nam. I pulled it from the locker beneath the forward vee-berth and opened it.

One by one, I handed him what he needed. "Here's my registration. Title's right here. And here's a Xerox copy of my hundred-ton passenger license."

He took the captain's license and studied it closely. I knew what he was going to ask, and he did: "Why a Xerox? Why not the real thing?"

"It was accidentally destroyed," I said. I was lying. It had been hanging on the wall of our little house on Elizabeth Street in Key West. And then the drug pirates set a little ignition bomb in the trunk of our old Chevy, planning to kill me. Only I hadn't started the car that night. My wife, Janet, had. The bomb had killed her and my two little twin boys, Ernest and Honor. After that, I couldn't bear to go back into that little shipbuilder's house where we had been so happy together.

So I never did.

Not even to pick up my captain's license.

"As you can see by the date there, chief, I have to renew my license in the next month or so, so I just decided to wait rather than apply for a duplicate."

"Hmm," he said, studying the papers, chewing

at the stub of a cigar. I started to say something, but he cut me off. "Captain MacMorgan, before you say another word, let me tell you something. I don't know if you and your buddy and that girl there are innocent parties in this or not. My cop instinct tells me you are—why didn't you just dump the dope overboard when you saw our chopper coming? But I don't take chances. We lose most of our arrests to sharpie lawyers as it is, so I'm telling you right now not to say another word until I formally arrest you and read you your rights."

"Arrest? Now wait a minute, dammit! We were just trying to help out!"

"Not another word, MacMorgan!"

The girl had been sitting silently at the little galley booth, watching and listening. When Chief Spears said the word "arrest" I saw her grimace. She rolled her eyes and shot me an "I told you not to call the Coast Guard!" look of disgust.

Spears marched the two of us topside, while O'Davis, in his best Irish brogue, stood trading sea stories with the other Coasties. They were already under his spell, caught up in the masculine comfort of rough talk and the Irishman's jokes. So they looked a little uneasy—reluctant, even—when Chief Spears gave them their orders. It was Coast Guard policy. They made the three of us lie spread-eagled on the aft deck.

"You are under arrest for violating federal laws," Chief Spears began. And then he recited our rights, the words "You have the right to remain silent . . ." spoken in a business monotone.

I felt a little ridiculous. No, more than ridiculous. I felt just a tad pissed off face down there on the deck of my own boat listening to a group of strangers tell me what I could and could not do. While Spears read us our rights, one of the other Coasties frisked us, taking the fine Gerber Magnum from the case on my belt. Another searched *Sniper*. When his search was completed, he came aft, a little excited. I couldn't see what he had found—but it was easy to guess.

"Damn, Chief, look what this guy was carrying on board!"

I heard the metallic *click* of the thirty-round clip being ejected. It was my Russian AK-47 assault rifle. When cruising, I keep it above the wheel in spring clips for ready access. There are plenty of pirates roaming the Florida Strait who'd like to see me disappear, and you never know when you might need some instant firepower. But of course, an automatic weapon is something less than legal. Especially a Russian automatic. No way to register and get a permit for it—so I had never even tried.

"Is this your weapon, Captain MacMorgan?" It was Spears. I heard the sound of a match being struck, and smelled the sour tobacco odor of his cheap cigar.

"Everything aboard this vessel is mine, Chief— except for the drugs. Like I told you." I rolled over to my back and sat up. I was between O'Davis and the girl. In the deck lights I could see the Irishman's broad face. He was smirking at me. And for good reason. It was a tricky situation. Ironic, too. Three different times I had been retained by an agency of the United States, as a freelance emissary. They needed a Florida Keys local with SEAL expertise to occasionally shake up the drug kingpins. They needed a man who knew when and how to kill; an outlaw working on the side of the law who could keep his mouth shut.

And here I was being arrested for suspicion of drug trafficking.

"So you admit that this weapon is yours?"

He held the assault rifle in one meaty hand. The hard hat was tilted back on his head, and his face was expressionless. Drugrunners are just about the only people afloat who carry automatic firepower. They have to—to protect themselves from the law and each other. And Spears thought he had me.

Without asking, I got to my feet. His men backed up slightly, weapons ready, giving themselves room to work. "Chief Spears," I said, "you've read me my rights, and I now freely waive them. I want to talk to you. But I want to talk in private."

He stared at me for a long moment, trying to figure out what ploy I was trying to work. Bribery? Coast Guard people love bribe offers—they can send you to prison for that much longer. So he decided to bite.

"Talk to me alone, huh?" He thought for a moment—but I could tell he had already made up his mind. He turned to his two men. "I'm going below with MacMorgan. You guys keep a close watch on these people."

They nodded knowingly. They'd be ready, all right—ready to cut me in two at the slightest sound of commotion.

He followed me down into the cabin at a safe distance. I paused at the little refrigerator.

"What are you getting there, MacMorgan?"

"Beer?"

He motioned to the booth. "You have a seat. Let's talk first."

The good ones don't take any chances. In the occupations of war and law enforcement, the briefest mistake can mean death. Spears was no perspiring, nervous-eyed rookie overreacting. He was just one cool professional hell-bent on keeping the odds in his favor. And I didn't blame him.

"Chief, there's a little round tin of snuff in my shirt pocket."

"Yeah, I can see the outline. Go ahead. Just keep your hands above the table."

I took out the Copenhagen and tapped a pinch between cheek and gum. He shook his head when I offered. "Used to chew when I played football for the Academy. Gave it up and took to cigars. Have to spit too much when you chew. It can mess up a boat."

"If you're not careful where you spit, it can."

I was beginning to get a reading on this man, Chief Petty Officer Spears, United States Coast Guard. It was unusual to be boarded by a CPO. They usually send a plain petty officer as boarding chief. He must have been aboard the *Royal Palm* for some special reason. What? No way of telling. What I had to know was that he could be trusted. I had vowed to tell no one of my activities with the United States government, knowing that if I ever got in trouble they would, in turn, disavow any knowledge of my activities. But I sure as hell didn't want to go through all the legal tanglings that went with being arrested for hauling drugs. He sat there across from me bulky and stumplike, chewing at his cigar, eyes trained on mine.

"Chief," I said, "I'm going to tell you the truth."

He shifted in his booth seat. "Sounds like a good start. How did you blow up that boat?"

"Just hold off on the cross-examination until I finish, okay?"

His dark eyes hardened momentarily. He didn't like being told what to do by a civilian. But he let it pass. "Okay. Fine, MacMorgan. Talk."

So I told him what had happened, detail by detail, leaving out only the girl. She had convinced O'Davis that she had reason for not making her story known to authorities, and that was good enough for me.

When I had finished, the chief rocked back and relit his cigar.

"Just up here on vacation, huh?"

"Came up from Key West to fish, drink beer, and relax."

He nodded, unconvinced. "Okay, MacMorgan. I listened to your story, now you listen to mine. Of the eighteen years I've been in the Coast Guard, the last ten have been the messiest, nastiest, and generally the biggest pain in the ass. This whole state has gone drug-crazy. Every Sunday boater has this dream of running to Jamaica or South America, picking up a load of grass, selling it, and retiring rich. And, damn it, a lot of them try. Now, this area here, the Ten Thousand Islands, has become the hottest drug drop spot in the nation. No law here, they figure. Nothing but deserted islands and empty sea. And since they shut down commercial fishing in the National Park, even some of the native-born fishing people are getting in on it. And I don't care how many men you have, you can't catch those good ol' boy fishermen in that jungle out there if they have a mind not to be caught." He paused, checked his watch, and munched on the cigar. "So you get the picture, MacMorgan? One hell of a lot of drugrunning going on here—some of it professional, but a hell of a lot of it amateur. See?"

I nodded. "But what's that got to do with us?"

He held up his hand. "Wait a minute. I'm not done. Okay, in the last eleven months four large vessels—all hauling drugs—have blown up in this area. 'Mysterious disappearances' the newspapers called them. But there's nothing mysterious about it when you find bits and pieces of hulls and bodies washing up on the beach. So that's why the brass ordered me out of my plush office and gave me sea duty again. I'm supposed to find out who's blowing up these boats. Do you know what I figure, MacMorgan?"

"You figure that the pros are getting real tired of the small fry cutting in on their territory. Or maybe there are two or three pro drug rings having a little friendly competition."

He stared at me in reappraisal. Law-enforcement people get real suspicious of private citizens with law-enforcement instincts. It makes them wary. Why should anyone besides cops think about criminal motives—unless they are lawmakers? Or lawbreakers.

"Absolutely right, MacMorgan." He eyed me shrewdly. "So I come out here to investigate a fifth explosion. And what do I find? I find you and your Irish friend, both of you looking like pro linebackers—or organized-crime hit men. You've got dope aboard, a girl who refuses to give us her name, and a Soviet-made assault rifle that I've only seen in the picture books. Now doesn't that sound just a little suspicious to you?"

It did. It did indeed. But for one thing. I said, "It brings us back to the original question—why didn't we just drop the dope and run? Why bother to report the explosion in the first place?"

Spears shrugged. "Damned if I know. Maybe

the guy you were trying to save got blown up by mistake. Maybe he was your brother. Or your friend. Or your priest." He shrugged again. "All I know, MacMorgan, is that I don't believe you're just John Q. Public out for a week of fishing. That little-blond-boy face of yours doesn't give away much—until you take a good look at the eyes. You're no stranger to this business, MacMorgan. Nothing reads right about you. No nervous jokes and clammy palms from you like with most of the rookies we nab. You and your buddy out there are just a little too cool for your own good."

"Maybe we're just secure in our innocence, Chief."

He snorted. "Even the innocent get real nervous when we come around, MacMorgan. They all figure they're guilty of something. So you're under arrest, MacMorgan. Face it."

He started to stand, but I stopped him. "Spears," I said, "I didn't want to go this far, but you give me no choice." He looked surprised at first. Then just amused.

"I know, I know," he said. "You're going to call some friend of yours and he's going to get you off, right? He's the mayor of some town, or maybe even a Congressman, and all he has to do is pull a few strings and we're going to let you go scot-free." His face hardened. And I could see that Chief Spears could be one bad man to have as an enemy. "Well, you're wrong, buster. The governor himself couldn't get you out of this. We're the feds, remember? So just come along nice and quiet."

"Fine," I said. "Have it your way. But before you cuff us, why not do us both a favor and make one simple phone call. It might save you some embarrassment."

He gazed at me stonily for a moment, then almost smiled. "And why should I?"

"Because you're right, Spears. I'm no stranger to this business."

"If this is going to be a confession, I want to get it on tape. With witnesses."

"It's no confession. You just overlooked one possibility. Maybe I'm not one of the bad guys."

It stopped him. Surprised him. He fiddled with his cigar some more. And then: "You say you have a phone number to back that up?"

I jotted the number down on a napkin. He seemed impressed by the area code—Washington, D.C. I followed him topside, where he took a hand radio from one of his men and contacted the *Royal Palm*. It took about twenty minutes for them to put the call through, and another twenty minutes for the orders to work their way down the chain of command. I couldn't hear what was said because his two armed men had the three of us sequestered away on the fighting deck. It was a long wait. The girl said nothing. She stood by the stern rail looking out toward the darkness of White Horse Key. She seemed to be in her own little world, opening her mouth only to yawn occasionally. O'Davis hummed his strange little Irish tune, "Tum-de-dum-dum," and paused to smile and wink at me from time to time. He knew what was going on.

Finally Chief Spears signaled me to follow him into *Sniper*'s cabin. No careful positioning and distance this time, and I knew that my federal friend Norman Fizer had come through. Spears didn't bother to sit. He made it quick. He stuck out his hand, and I took it. Firm dry handshake.

"Story confirmed, MacMorgan. I don't know what you do—and I don't want to know. But some very big people got upset with me when they heard I had placed you under arrest."

I nodded and said nothing. His blunt face studied me, expressionless. "What, no cry of outrage? No demand for an apology from me to you and your friends?"

"Not hardly, Chief. You were just doing your job. And from what I saw, you do your job damn efficiently. No apology necessary."

He smiled briefly, extended his hand again, and then said, "One more thing, Captain Mac-Morgan."

"What's that?"

He took the stub of the cigar from his mouth, eyed it evilly, then stuffed it into his shirt pocket. "I'd like to take you up on that offer to have a dip of snuff. I'd forgotten how much I missed it until I saw you take one. . . ."

5

The island was set apart from Gullivan Bay, totally isolated, yet close enough to open sea to be edged with sweeping white beach, Australian pines, and coconut palms leaning in windward strands. It was a tough island to get to. One natural unmarked channel snaked its way past mangrove islands and shoal water, and oyster bars guarded the mouth of the channel.

It was some pretty island to see in the light of a clear June morning. Gumbo-limbo trees stood atop the swollen lift of Indian shell mounds, and the rest of the island was a thatch of citrus trees, mahogany, and ficus. Land birds cackled from the bushes.

You couldn't even see the neat line of white clapboard buildings until you were right on them. But they were there. Just as the girl had said.

Because the channel was so narrow, O'Davis

was forward on the bow testing the water with a fourteen-foot pushpole I normally carried in the Whaler when fishing for bonefish. He wore khaki cutoffs and no shirt. The muscles of his calves bulged above his ragged tennis shoes, and his shoulders corded as he plumbed the water. With his red hair and woolly blond leg and back thatch, the Irishman looked like some heather-born gnome who had been transformed and braced by oak four-by-sixes.

"Coupla points ta port, Yank!"

Steering from the flybridge, I made the necessary weave that kept us in the channel. The water was a roiled green, stained with the humic and tannic acids of this Florida backcountry, and the air was pungent with the herbaceous odor of mangrove and cactus and the iodine sharpness of open sea.

Suddenly, O'Davis stopped working the pole. Something on the island seemed to capture his attention. And then I saw it too. About a hundred yards away on the white sand beach. And it captured my attention, too.

"What was that ya were sayin' back in Key West, brother MacMorgan?" O'Davis yelled up at me. "No women in the Ten Thousand Islands, didn't ya' say?" His face was contorted into a huge grin. "I'm a-tellin' ya, they find me like moths find a flame, Yank! Look at 'em, mate—ain't they somethin'?"

They were something indeed.

A half dozen women lay on towels and blankets, naked on the sand in the morning sun. Oil glistened on their bodies. They were of different ages, late teens to mid-thirties it seemed, all in fine shape. A tall brunette walked from the water toward the island, her buttocks swaying. There was no white swath of bikini stripe on any of the women. They were no strangers to his kind of sunbathing. I expected them to get up and run at our approach—or at least cover themselves. But they didn't. They just lay there in the sun, oiled and brown and aloof, hair and bodies tawny as young lionesses.

O'Davis had completely abandoned his soundings now. He stood on the bow, mouth agape, enjoying the scenery. It was okay with me. We had a strong incoming spring tide, and the water eddied around the shoal areas making the channel easy to read now.

The girl had told us about the island after the Coast Guard had left us the night before. We were all dead tired, and I wasn't up to trying to navigate strange backwaters by moonlight. So we had anchored off White Horse Key, sat on the stern with drinks, and watched Chief Spears's *Royal Palm* salvage the drug flotsam and search for survivors. It was tedious work and gruesome. The Coasties aren't paid all that well. And they work hard for what they do get. We didn't watch for long. The girl seemed to be drifting deeper and deeper into a world of her own despair. She still refused to let us have her transported to a hospital for observation. She said *Sniper*'s hull had conked her on the head—but not very hard. So when we retreated into the privacy of *Sniper*'s cabin she sat on the gold cloth couch seat across from the galley, moping. The jazz station in Fort Myers had signed off, and WKWF in Key West had taken a sudden acid-rock jag, so Westy ambled over to the radio, switched it off, and gave me a wink.

"Do ye not think, Captain MacMorgan, that the three of us could produce some better music than that?"

I saw what he was doing—trying to cheer the girl up; maybe relieve her of the memories of the last couple of days.

"I do, Captain O'Davis, I do—if you don't sing along, that is."

I watched the girl. She actually let a smile cross her face.

The Irishman put his hands on his hips and looked at me gruffly. "So ya think I canna sing, ya big ugly brute! Well, we'll let this fine young lady here be the judge—but first, let's fill our glasses!"

So O'Davis filled our glasses ceremoniously. After my stay in Mariel Harbor, Cuba, I had just about had my fill of Hatuey beer. Not because it isn't fine beer—it is. But because of where it is made—Havana. I had come away from Mariel with no love for Castro's little commie haven, so now I was drinking that fine Tuborg beer from bottles. It was a silly little protest. But I've made silly protests before, and I expect I'll make them again.

So it was Tuborg for me, dark Guinness stout for the Irishman, and more peach brandy (minus the coffee) for the girl. O'Davis played what he said was an old Gaelic drinking game. We would all take turns singing a song of our choice. If the person who started the song forgot any of the words, he or she had to drain his glass.

It was the sort of game where everybody loses—or wins, depending on how you look at it.

But it worked.

After a shy beginning, the girl began joining in with O'Davis's endless repertoire of drinking and whaling songs, and she actually began a few of her own. At somewhere between eighteen and twenty-one, her taste in music was not nearly as limited as I would have guessed. She did a pretty good version of "Heartbreak Hotel." And several glasses of brandy later, when her turn came again, she added a musky "As Time Goes By," in a smoky contralto. It was a perfect choice for her. She had the same fine, unusually angular face as Bacall; the same torch singer's voice. And when she finally forgot the words of the last verse, she swore with a fervor that might have done justice to Bacall herself. The fact that Bacall never sang "As Time Goes By" seemed to make no difference at all in her delivery.

It was about an hour into the game that she

finally broke. Westy and I had been trying to harmonize on the old whaling song "Row Away." She began to laugh so hard that she spilled her drink. We both stooped to pick up the glass at the same time, and we bumped heads mightily.

And that made her laugh even harder, tears rolling, heavy breasts heaving beneath the blue plaid shirt.

Westy and I recognized it at the same time. The thick laughter was suddenly edged with hysteria.

She took two steps backward, holding her stomach, face tilted upward, and plopped drunkenly onto the couch.

And her laughter became a rage of tears. O'Davis went to her, but she slapped him away, then hid her face in her hands, sobbing. We exchanged looks.

I grabbed his arm and pulled his ear close to my face.

"Remember that bucket?"

"Aye. Yer thinkin' that peach brandy might be a-seekin' some fresh air."

"Shrewd, O'Davis. Shrewd."

He moved quickly from the cabin. I tore a handful of paper towels from the roll above the sink and handed it to the girl. She took them reluctantly and wiped her eyes. She began to say something, but grabbed her stomach instead. Her face turned pale, and the Irishman arrived with the bucket just in time. Nothing feminine about upchucking. She coughed and sweated and spewed. The convulsions seemed both physical and emotional; a two-in-the-morning cathartic that wracked her brain and body. It left her leached, weak—but she seemed to feel one hell of a lot better.

And she actually began to talk.

We were her two confidants. She included Westy and me equally. It happens that way—even in a short period of time—when you have suffered, drunk, and sung together.

Westy had gotten a towel and loaded it with ice. She held it on her forehead. I had her feet propped up with a pillow, and her head lay on my lap on the little couch. At first, she seemed uncomfortable with the close contact, but finally she relaxed, settling back, one hand thrown up behind her head.

"Damn," she said, wiping her face wearily.

"Brandy will do that to you. By the way, I don't even know your name."

"Hmm?" She coughed weakly. "What's in a name?"

"Convenience, for one thing," I answered. "I want to know who to offer the aspirins to tomorrow morning."

Hers was a weak, sardonic smile. "Shit, why wait? My head's pounding already. Some wild night, huh? And my name's Barbara."

"Barbie for short."

"No."

There was some bitterness in the way she said it. "So it's Barbara."

"Yeah. I don't know why men always want to shorten a woman's name into something cute and easy. Maybe it's because that's the way they want women to be."

"We're all bastards," I said. She didn't miss the sarcasm. And neither did Westy. Playing the mediator, he jumped in.

"Except for meself an' this scarred-up brute," he said hastily.

She studied us both for a second, appraising, ready to jump back into her shell again. The weak grin told me she had decided otherwise. "I guess you two guys have been pretty nice to me. And I appreciate it. I really do. Hey, Irish—how about those aspirins, huh?"

O'Davis nodded regally, like an English butler. "Immediately, Barbara. An' me friends call me Westy."

"That's why I call him O'Davis," I added.

She chuckled. "You two are funny—for older guys. Always grousing at each other like you're enemies or somethin'. But you're really good friends. Like Bob Hope and that other old guy— I think he died recently—in those old *Road* pictures. I used to watch their movies on TV. Used to really make me laugh."

Her green eyes were glassy for a moment, child-like, far, far away. Westy brought aspirins and water, bringing her out of it. I watched her drink down the water, milk-white throat veined with blue, face still pale. She sniffed and handed back the glass.

"God," she said. "What a night."

"Things can get wild in the Ten Thousand Islands," I said. "A lot of wilderness and not much law. I'm kind of wondering what brings you down here."

A natural wariness seemed to overtake her momentarily. But then she relaxed. She said, "It's no big deal, really. I had some problems back home. Detroit. I grew up there right on the outskirts of the Motor City. Suburbanville, I'll tell you. You ever been to Detroit?"

I shook my head. "It's never been one of my driving desires."

"I've been there, lass," O'Davis said. "No offense, Barbara, me dear, but Detroit sorta looks like the devil decided to go into the automobile business."

"Yeah," she said. "The place really stank. Smog, slush, and drugs. One hell of a good place for high school kids to get bored and do crazy things. The crazy thing I did was marry my high school sweetheart. He was a two-hundred-pound All State fullback with the brain of a grade school kid. Everybody had spoiled him: his parents, his coaches, and his teachers. He expected the same thing from me. And I went along with it for a few years. I supported him and put myself through nursing school all at the same time. I smiled when he came home all beered up from drinking with his ex-teammates, and I helped him into bed after he'd gotten his jollies slappin' me around awhile. I used to think that was a wife's job—putting up with her husband's guff. God knows, my mother went through it long enough."

She sniffed, took another sip of water, and I noticed that her hands were shaking.

"So the divorce was inevitable," I finished.

There was a bitter look on her face, and her green eyes narrowed.

"You're damn right it was, buster. One night he punched me a little too hard. Broke a couple of my ribs and punctured a lung. I spent the next few weeks in a hospital. Luckily, there's a group up there that specializes in rehabilitating battered wives. The group is called SELF—Self-Education and Liberation for Feminists—and talking to those women was worth the beating I took. It changed my life. They helped me realize that I had nothing to feel guilty about—that it was my pea-brained husband who had the problems. They helped me understand that I was a person, not just some punchboard put on this earth for some man's amusement." She sighed. "I just wish to hell I had run into SELF a couple of years earlier."

"And that brings us back to why you're here on the west coast of Florida in the Ten Thousand Islands."

"Right," she aid. "Hey, Irish—I mean, Westy. Any chance of getting a small glass of milk?"

She sat up and rubbed her stomach gently, sore, probably, from the brandy-induced illness. When Westy handed her the glass, she drank it down in one go. The milk left a thin curve of mustache on her upper lip, and it made her look very young and vulnerable.

"Where was I? Oh, yeah—SELF is a federally funded program, and they sponsor these Awareness Retreats all around the country. Living in Detroit, I've always been kinda fascinated with the idea of living by the sea. Sounds weird, I guess, but I've just always wanted to do it. So, a few years ago, SELF was allowed to take over an old research station down here on a little island called Mahogany Key. You heard of it?"

I shook my head. "Maybe. A long time ago, didn't they do research on the tarpon spawn up there? I've never seen the place—just heard about it."

"It was something like that; some kinda fish research. But SELF took it over, like I said. It's part of the National Park, I guess. So, like at the rest of the Awareness Retreats, SELF sponsors real interesting classes on all sorts of stuff. Marine biology and birds and stuff like that. Real interesting. We stay right there on the island, have seminars, exercise classes, learn to meditate. I'll tell you, it's been just great."

"So how did you happen to get mixed up with the drugrunners on the boat that went down?"

She looked at me sharply. "I was just getting to that, okay?"

"Sorry, Barbara. Didn't mean to rush you. It's just that I'm interested, that's all. If you don't feel up to talking anymore, that's fine."

She gave me a weak smile. "Guess I'm a little touchy, huh? They're trying to teach me how to relate to men again, but that's been the hardest part for me. It's like every man I see, it's that creep of a husband of mine I see instead."

"Easy ta understand, lass. There are some real bastards around—male and female alike. But if ye don't want ta talk about it . . ."

"No," she said quickly, "I do. I need to get it out of me. Okay—SELF has this self-awareness project where you learn basic survival; you know, how to live off the land—stuff like that. It's a two-week course. And at the end of the two weeks, they take you out and drop you off on an island alone. It's called 'solo.' It's supposed to help your self-confidence. Well, I was on my solo out there on White Horse Key, when this big boat came up—called the *Blind Luck*, filled with all these greasy, ratty-looking guys. One of the rules of the SELF solo is that you're not supposed to talk to anybody. They say you can learn a hell of a lot in perfect silence. So these guys started getting real nasty when I refused to talk to them. So they just kidnapped me—simple as that. They forced me to get into their skiff with them and ride back to the . . . the . . ."

I could see her struggling to fight back the tears.

"We can guess the rest, Barbara."

She wiped her hand roughly across her face. "That's right. And you'll guess exactly right. Those bastards. But . . ." She hesitated, thinking, a look of fresh awareness in her eyes. "But I guess it doesn't matter, huh?"

She wasn't making much sense now, and when I started to say something she cut me off.

"It's like what they were teaching us back on the island—no outside influence has any . . . what did they call it? Yeah—no outside influence has any effect on your life unless you let it. That's right. Unless you react to it!" She looked supremely comforted by her own words. She sat there peaked, tired—but suddenly serene. And I had to admit that what she said made sense.

O'Davis patted her shoulder gently. "Yer right, child. Yer absolutely right."

She sniffed and looked up at him. Her eyes were teary, but there was a slight smile on her face. "To hell with them, then! To hell with what happened. They may have had me physically, but it doesn't make a goddamn bit of difference, does it? It doesn't make any difference because they didn't have *me*. I was never really involved at all! They might just as well have had a picture of me, huh?"

She looked at us quickly for a confirmation; eyes bright, believing, but wanting us to agree, too. It was pretty touching. I didn't even know this girl. But she was reaching across to us for help.

"You're damn right it doesn't make any difference," I said, grinning.

She got up, found the tuning switch on the radio, and dialed in the all-night rock station in Naples. The jock was playing something slow and syrupy with a lot of sax and guitar licks. The lead singer was doing a low wail that was supposed to pass for lyrics. She stood facing the radio for a while, absorbing the music, caught up in the silence of her own thoughts. And then her hips began to sway gently, feet moving in the slow flow of the music. The cabin light caught the short blond hair, highlighting it and turning it to spun glass. Shadows on her face made cheeks and nose finer, more angular, better-defined in relation to the full mouth. Her eyes were half closed and her head swayed, as she moved her buttocks in perfect time beneath the cutoff shorts. The Irishman and I exchanged looks. To any male animal she would be an enticing package of female pulchritude—femininely sinewy yet soft. But like some of those lithe bikini-clad girls you see on any Florida beach, all youth and preoccupied aloofness, this one too just filled you with vague stirrings and vaguer regrets. We both sighed at the same time, then smiled at the ridiculous thoughts we were both entertaining.

O'Davis got up and retrieved beer from the refrigerator and handed me mine.

"Gettin' a bit late for old-timers like you an'

me, eh, brother MacMorgan?" he said, just softly enough for the girl not to hear.

"Get me my cane and I'll hobble in to bed—after another Tuborg, that is."

The girl danced on in her own little world, back to us, unself-conscious yet withdrawn. When I got up to get our final beer, she stopped suddenly and looked at us both.

"You two can drop me off on the island tomorrow, right?"

I nodded. "Mahogany Key? Sure. We're heading in to Dismal Key, and it's not far from there."

She looked troubled for a moment. "You know, like I said—it's all women. I'm not sure if they'll let men . . ."

"Don't worry," I interrupted. "We'll just drop you off and leave. No problem."

I crossed in front of her, and she took my arm, looking up into my eyes. "Hey, no offense, you know. You two guys have been pretty damn nice to me. Saved my life maybe. I feel like I owe you something."

I could have taken the remark in a dozen different ways. But I chose not to. I just wanted to get this beautiful creature off *Sniper* and get back to our vacation. Aside from the primal stirrings, I have no real interest in hustling pretty little strangers into the sack. And I sure as hell didn't want to spend much time on an island full of raving feminists.

I winked at her, trying to make it a brotherly

wink. "Just remember what you said a while ago—about outside influences."

She nodded and grinned. Standing beside me she seemed very small but no longer vulnerable. "I will," she said. "Adversity, depression—all that bad stuff. It's just like a phone ringing. You can choose to answer it and suffer. Or you can choose not to answer and just forget it. And I'm goddamn well going to forget it. . . ."

6

Westy and I watched the sun-oiled women on the beach as we approached. Mahogany Key was iridescent in the morning light, and the women lay on blankets in the sand, lovely and aloof as young lions. I could smell the heat of cactus and mangroves as we neared, and then the fruity odor of suntan lotion.

"The dock's around on the other side."

It was the girl, Barbara. She seemed to have recovered fully from her drinking bout of the night before. She came climbing up the ladder to *Sniper*'s flybridge, her blond hair neatly combed and parted in the middle. She wore the same cutoff shorts, but had changed into one of my T-shirts. She had tied the excess material into a knot above her belly button. She was braless and filled out the T-shirt better than I would have expected.

"Feeling better?"

She nodded curtly, a new formality about her. "Guess I drank too much, huh? I feel pretty damn silly." She had a nervous mannerism, playing with her fingernails.

"Sometimes drinking's good medicine. And Barbara, you weren't silly last night. Not at all. And it wouldn't have mattered if you had been. I make it a practice to be silly every now and again myself."

"Oh. Hmm." She looked up at me and smiled. "Thanks."

O'Davis looked up, noticing her, and grinned and waved. She waved back.

"You guys *are* a funny pair, you know."

"Funny weird? Or funny funny?"

"Funny nice. A nice sort of strange, you know? Kind of odd for older guys to be roaming around on a boat like this. You seem like the type who ought to be planted behind a desk running a big company or something, and pinching the secretaries."

"Thanks a hell of a lot."

"I didn't mean you *are* like that. But at your age . . ."

I chuckled. "The only reason we seem so old is because you're so young, Barbara. And I like roaming around in this boat. And so does O'Davis. We like it, so that's what we do. Okay?"

"I didn't mean anything by it." She stuck out her hand. "Friends again?"

"Absolutely," I said.

The winding channel filtered into an oval bay behind the island. A low bank of mangroves to the west protected it from the open Gulf. The girl stood beside me on the flybridge, watching me maneuver *Sniper* through the shoalwater. There was something I wanted to talk to her about, and I decided there wasn't much time left.

"So you've recovered, huh?"

She sighed. "Yeah. Yeah, I have. It all sort of seems like a bad dream, now. Like it happened to a stranger. In a way, I guess it did. No one can really hurt you unless you pay the price of bitterness. And those bastards aren't worth it. Besides, I've got two more weeks on Mahogany Key. It's plenty to look forward to."

"And after that?"

She thought for a moment. "After that, maybe I'll become an instructor for SELF. I've got my RN degree, and they always have openings for nurses."

"Sounds like a big organization."

"Not really. Small—but top-quality. It's changed my life. And for the better. Women really do have a tough time of it, Dusky. Like that album cover a long time back called women the slaves of the world. Well, it is that way because we let it be that way. That's what SELF teaches us. We have to start recognizing ourselves as valuable individuals, and if we do, the world will come around. Eventually."

"Makes sense to me," I said.

"Does it really?"

I smiled. "Even at my age."

She laughed. It was a deep, husky laugh and good to the ears. It was the first time I had heard her laugh without the edge of hysteria.

"Look, Barbara, there's something I've wanted to ask you about."

She shuffled her feet, seemingly nervous. "Yeah?"

"Yeah—and don't look at me that way. It's nothing too personal. It's about that boat."

"The *Blind Luck*?"

"Yeah, if you don't mind."

She thought for a moment. "I don't see how any good can come of it, but if you want. . . ." She shifted her weight, standing.

"You were aboard for what? Two days?"

"Something like that."

"I was hoping you could tell me what the men aboard were like." And then I added hastily, "Maybe you can throw a little light onto why someone would have blown up their vessel."

"Maybe it was just an accident."

I stared at her for a moment. "If you don't want to talk about it, just say so."

She shook her head wearily. "Okay, okay. I guess I owe you at least that—but God knows why you're interested. There were six or seven of them aboard. All pretty young. There was no real leader, I don't think, because they argued and fought all the time. No order to their routines. They slept when they wanted, ate when they wanted, and they all seemed to be real heavy into drugs."

"You say that like you disapprove."

"Of drugs?" She snorted. "It's because I do disapprove. I saw what they did to my older brother. And besides, it's the one thing SELF really preaches against. Their philosophy is that a woman can't stand on her own two feet if she uses a stimulant as a crutch. I'm not saying some of the women don't occasionally share a joint, but the organization is against heavy use. And so am I. Like I said, I watched drugs destroy my brother. And it wasn't a very pretty sight."

"You said they argued a lot. What about?"

"Oh, stupid stuff. Like kids. You know that mentality: spoiled little brats in adult bodies. I pretty much gathered they'd been to South America and picked up a load, and that they were sick and tired of each other's company."

"So why were they waiting around off White Horse Key?"

She shook her head. "Waiting to meet somebody, I guess. I really don't know. Maybe someone to help unload the stuff." She stopped for a moment, thinking.

"You look like something bothers you."

"Well, something strange *did* happen while I was aboard. Maybe it's important, maybe it's not. The second night, the night I finally jumped overboard, I heard what sounded like another boat come up. I was below, so I can't really be sure. But I heard strange voices, and the boat kept jarring against something like we were tied up to another boat."

"And then what?"

She shrugged. "And then nothing. Our engines started again, and we were underway for a while, and that's when I got free, grabbed my lifejacket, and jumped overboard."

"But you got free just about where you started. Didn't you say you were doing your solo on White Horse Key?"

"Yeah," she said, perplexed. "It is kind of strange that they would have gone to meet a boat rather than letting the boat come to them—if it was the pickup boat. Frankly, I didn't know where in the hell we were. I just knew I wanted out. So I jumped. And then I saw your boat coming along, and I tried to flag you down. Next thing I knew, I was lying on your deck bare-chested with one hell of a headache." She smiled, slightly embarrassed, it seemed. "You know, that's what impressed me about you two."

"What's that, Barbara?"

"You kept me covered. Most guys would have stood there gawking." She made an oddly shy motion toward her breasts. "You know, most girls want big boobs. But believe me, once you have them they become a liability real quick. You guys don't know how lucky you are."

"Saves on shopping," I said.

She grinned. A fine girlish grin. "Anyway, you two have been real sweet." She got way up on her tiptoes and gave me a kiss on the cheek. Soft lips, moist. "And I'm going to see if I can't get permission to show you around the island. Most of the girls enjoy walking around naked, and that's why they don't allow men ashore."

"So I see," I said, nodding toward the beach. The women were slowly ambling toward cover at our approach. The expressions on their faces were indifferent and slightly perturbed at being bothered. "I'm surprised the locals aren't out here all the time with binoculars."

"Oh, we get some of that. But not much, because the place is so isolated. And besides," she said, a sharp glint in her eye, "the SELF staff knows how to handle intruders. It's a private island. And they're pretty good at keeping it that way. . . ."

I brought *Sniper* around behind Mahogany Key. The dense foliage that screened the front of the island now broke into an airy clearing of swept shell and sand, and white clapboard buildings. The paths that led from building to building were neatly outlined in old whelk shells, and hibiscus and jasmine trees bloomed red and blue and white along the paths. The flag of Florida hung below the American flag in the limp June morning.

"How many women are on this island?"

The girl eyed the settlement anxiously, obviously happy to be back. "About a hundred, I guess. Maybe more, but it seems like less. You get to know everyone pretty quickly, because we all eat together."

"You all don't take the same classes?"

"Not really. Except for maybe the self-image and the meditation classes, but even there we're split up into groups. Isn't it a beautiful place?"

It was indeed. Before the concrete poured-to-form money mongers arrived in Florida, there was a short period in the early 1900s when craftsmen built houses of wood and tin and coquina rock. The houses were built with grace, solid as ships, and they'll probably stand long after the condominium and stucco grotesqueries are ground to dust. And Mahogany Key seemed to have benefited from the best of that era. The buildings were squat and simple, with the whitewashed effulgence of the tropics. Only the docks were new: built of treated pilings and pressurized planking, they were broad and substantial, like all government docks. Three bright-yellow Mitchell skiffs with small outboards were moored in the shallows. On the outside of the dock's T was a broad-beamed pontoon boat abused with hauling foodstuffs and fuel for the island's generators. Obviously, everything they used on the island had to be shipped in. On the inside of the dock, tied off in deep water, was a twenty-foot Shamrock, a classic of small-boat design. I had to admire their taste in boats. I had run a Shamrock only once before—

but fell in love with it. With its 302 inboard, top speed is right at forty, and with its heavy skeg keel the brass prop and tiller are practically untouchable. In the shoalwater area of the Ten Thousand Islands with its mixture of open sea and treacherous oyster bars, the Shamrock was a perfect choice.

It took only one of the women on the island to recognize Barbara for the rest of them to come on the run to greet her. Somewhere an old dinner bell rang a message, and the buildings emptied.

"Looks like you're pretty popular here, lady."

She sniffed, and her eyes were brimming. "Isn't it great? Those women . . . it's only been a couple of weeks, and they're already like . . . sisters."

"In that case, you'd better grab whatever you want aboard and get down there to greet them. If they all try to jump onto my boat, we'll sink."

I brought *Sniper* in gently, nosing her up behind the pontoon boat, then stopped her with a reverse thrust on engines. Westy was ready with the lines, and had her snubbed off and bumpered by the time I got down to the fighting deck. He came up beside me, arms folded across his thick chest, a wry look on his face.

"Will ye look at all the women, brother Mac-Morgan," he said.

"Every possible shape and size."

"An' all that huggin' and kissin' goin' on—why, it's disgustin' it is." He shook himself.

"I can see it bothers you."

"What I'm tryin' ta understand is how they kin keep their hands off me! Look at the tall auburn one there, ever so handsome, tryin' ta pretend she doesn't notice me. Ah, the poor girl—already hopelessly in love." He nodded his head as if burdened with some great knowledge. "What amazin' self-control the lass has, Dusky."

"And what an amazing actress she is. Pretending she couldn't care less."

O'Davis waved his hand as if shooing a fly. "You'll see, Yank. Yer sarcasm is wasted."

There were a number of beautiful women in the crowd, but the one the Irishman had mentioned was striking indeed. Even dressed as she was in simple white baggy pants and jersey, she had an aristocratic air. Nothing aloof or affected—just that look of total self-confidence that makes certain people natural sovereigns. Her hair was autumn-colored and swayed behind her in a loose ponytail. She was a woman of length and lines; the sort you see on yacht-club tennis courts, or on the covers of certain magazines. She walked with her arms folded across the loose folds of her jersey.

"Shame it is, Yank, to break the heart of the likes of that," he said sadly. "But Wes O'Davis, meself I'm speakin' of, is not the marryin' kind."

"Just be kind when you let her down, O'Davis—but you'd better make it quick before she ignores you right out of her life."

The crowd of women parted as she approached.

Barbara stood tearfully in the middle of the throng
on the dock. Her smile broadened as the woman
with the auburn hair approached, and she went
running to her and they hugged. The nobility on
the face of the auburn-haired woman melted into
a warm girlish smile. They stood away from each
other, hugged again, and then Barbara began to
talk. She wore my T-shirt, and she had the old life
vest slung over one shoulder. She said she wanted
it as a keepsake. The other women on the dock
stood back and watched happily. Obviously the
woman with auburn hair was one of their leaders.
And just as obviously, they all knew that something had gone wrong on Barbara's solo.

"I think it's time we made our exit, O'Davis."

The Irishman conjured up a look of shock.
"What, Dusky? An' leave all these lovely ladies?
Me boy, ye've spent too much time alone."

"You grab the lines and we'll get under way."

Anything else Westy had to say was drowned
out by the roar of *Sniper*'s twin diesels. Reluctantly, he went to free bow and stern lines. Barbara looked surprised when she saw that we were
about to leave. And actually disappointed. She
said something hurriedly to the woman with the
auburn hair. And for the first time, the woman
turned to face me, locking in on my eyes. Hers
was a face with impact—not so much beautiful as
it was singular and lovely. She tilted her head
slightly, said something to Barbara, and Barbara

came toward *Sniper* on a light trot, hips swaying in an awkward girlish gait.

"Ye see, Yank, the princess there won't let me leave!" O'Davis said gaily.

"She looks smarter than that."

"Ah, she's only human, Dusky."

"And that makes it even harder to understand why she would be interested in the likes of you."

The Irishman just chuckled to himself and began to hum his strange little tune, "tum-de-dum-dum," as he threw a couple of clove hitches, retying us.

"Dusky, it's okay! You can come ashore and look around!" Barbara stood on the dock looking like a kid at Christmas. Apparently this was some kind of unprecedented honor. The other women of Mahogany Key looked on, surprised, but not necessarily happy about it.

"Actually, we're in kind of a hurry."

"And how could we turn down such a charmin' invitation?" O'Davis interrupted loudly, making a sweeping gesture with his thick right arm. He looked up and gave me a private wink. 'We'd be pleased to tour yer lovely island!"

So what do you do? I shut down *Sniper*'s engines, stuffed the keys into my pocket in some unconscious mood of mistrust, and went ashore. Except for Barbara and the woman with auburn hair, the others moved off the dock at our approach. They walked a little too quickly down the shell path that led toward the whitewashed island houses. Something bothered me about the way they paired off. They were women of varied ages, most between twenty-one and thirty-five it seemed, many of them scantily dressed in shorts and bikini tops, and some damn attractive. But they walked away from us, oiled legs gliding, hips swaying, holding hands or bumping shoulders like school-girls. And their was an exclusiveness to their pair-ing that disturbed me. Watching them, I felt an uneasiness, something that offended some sub-merged animal instinct. And then I knew: these were the physically and emotionally battered, women who, for reasons good or bad, had grown to hate men and finally had taken love and refuge in the safest of harbors—homosexuality.

I watched them walk away, lithe and oiled and lovely, buttocks and breasts like warm fortresses, solitary women with hair of blond and brown and black, shoulders held proudly erect.

"Ah, brother MacMorgan, let's not be rude now."

"Hum? What?"

I hadn't even noticed Barbara and the woman with auburn hair come up beside me.

"Oh, I'm sorry. I was thinking."

The woman with the auburn hair seemed not— or chose not—to hear me. She was lovely indeed. She stood looking into my eyes, only an inch or two shorter than I. She was so striking that it took me a long moment to notice her eyes. They were the softest of soft blue, and each just the tiniest bit off center, so that she seemed to be focusing on the edges of her fine cover-girl nose.

She extended her hand, a look on her face of neither approval nor disapproval. "Welcome to Mahogany Key, Captain MacMorgan," she said, her voice almost warm, her handshake firm, dry, and hard.

7

Her name was Saxan. Saxan Benton.

Unusual name for an unusual woman.

She was one of those ageless ones. At nine, nineteen, or forty-nine, she would always and forever be a classic beauty. As she walked Westy and me across the island, I tried to get a reading on her. But it was tough. She said little about herself. Her voice was clear, woodwind-like, and edged with the slightest of accents. French, perhaps. Or a light mixture of French and rich. There was a Southhampton roundness to her vowels, and the same careful use of syntax you hear at the ritzy lawn parties on Long Island or in Beverly Hills. There was a natural aloofness to her, but none of that hateful contrived air of superiority. She made conversation—conversation didn't flow from her. She was the hostess and we were strangers being briefly entertained—that sort of polite congeniality. Saxan Benton walked with her arms folded lightly across her chest, the length of her strides almost matching mine. She plied us with questions, the friendly kind, and she listened well, drawing into her own little world again when she came across some plant or tree or land snail that interested her. She would say their names out loud, but to herself, and then add the Latin name—not to impress, but more to firm them in her own mind, like an exercise.

"An interesting lantana here," she said, stooping to touch a small shrub.

"Very interestin'," O'Davis said, exchanging looks with me. She didn't even hear him, concentrating on the tiny flowers the way she was, and the Irishman seemed to think that kind of funny.

"Saxan is a botanist," Barbara said. She had been walking Mohogany Key with us, eyeing the auburn-haired older woman with an obvious fondness. "She took her master's at Smith."

"Ah, Smith," said O'Davis. I gave him a look of warning. This wasn't the place for his dry Irish sense of humor.

"*Camara* of the verbena family," Saxan said softly. "The flower clusters display all three of the common colors—pink, orange, and yellow. It's rather unusual to see all three colors on one shrub. The petals are deadly poison, of course."

"Of course!" said O'Davis.

Without standing, the woman turned her face up. "Are you interested in plants, Mr. O'Davis?"

"Love broccoli, hate peas, Miss Benton."

I didn't expect her controlled expression to fall from her face the way it did. The laughter tumbled from her. Her eyes, blue and slightly off center, glistened. And in that moment, she seemed wonderfully open and vulnerable and human. And in that same moment, I began to like this new woman. Very much.

"Your friend is very funny, Captain Mac-Morgan."

"He's a regular circus, Ms. Benton. And my name's Dusky."

She stood, dusting her palms together. "Okay, then—Dusky it is."

"And Westy?"

She nodded and smiled at the Irishman. "And Westy—if you two will call me Saxan?" She laughed self-consciously as we walked with her up the Indian shell mound toward the largest white clapboard building on the island. "You see, I'm afraid my father was a terrible Anglophile. Was absolutely fascinated with the English— which is odd, since he was born in Paris."

"Would a been much odder had he been Irish," O'Davis said darkly.

"Yes, that's true! My father wanted to name me Britton, but my mother insisted on a compromise, so it was Saxon, with an o, and then Saxan with an a, because it seemed more feminine."

"And you agree?"

The smile left her face as suddenly as it had

appeared. "Unfortunately, the only thing my father and I ever agreed upon was that plants are extremely interesting. You see, he was a botanist, too." Abruptly, she changed the subject. It was like slamming the door on her past. Case closed. Period.

It took us the better part of an hour to tour the island. It was impressive, indeed. Mahogany Key had been the private retreat of a millionaire Chicago sportsman in the early 1920s. It had been donated to an Illinois university after the Depression and converted into a research center for the nation's marine biologists. When the upkeep became too high for the university, it was given to the government, and except for being used for some commando training during the war years, it was allowed to fall into disrepair.

"The place was an absolute wreck when the government decided to lease the island to us," Saxan Benton said. She sat behind her desk in her office on the big house on the mound. The office was surprisingly Spartan: metal desk and chair, one old couch for visitors. On the wall were photographs of island birds: ospreys in flight, and a fine shot of skimmers, their orange beaks trailing in a mirror sea. The office smelled of old wood and plaster, and of the woman herself: a light sandalwood musk.

"Your organization—SELF, was it?—must have some money behind it to have restored the place so well," I said. The Irishman and I sat on the couch across from her. Barbara had excused herself to visit with her other friends on the island and get back to classes.

"I wish that were true," she said. Her hands played absently with a blue Flair pen, and I noticed for the first time that she wore absolutely no jewelry. "Fortunately, HEW provides the financial backing—some of it in matching funds. We just supply the workforce."

"Ye mean you women did all this?" O'Davis said incredulously. "Why, the place is a paradise."

"Don't be so surprised, Mr. O'Davis," she said shortly. Saxan Benton was not amused this time. But with her off-center eyes, the look she gave him seemed anything but fierce; only endearing. "That's what Self-Education and Liberation for Feminists is all about. I find the idea that only men can be competent carpenters, plumbers, and electricians to be totally absurd. And I think we've proved it here— and at our other centers around the country."

"Me dear, I didn't mean to imply—"

"And I am not 'your dear,' Mr.—"

"Hold it, hold it, time out," I said. I was as surprised as the Irishman that she had flared so quickly. The conversation was taking an unhealthy turn, and there was nothing to be gained by any of it. Besides, I wanted to learn more about Mahogany Key before they kicked our butts off. I had dealt with a frighteningly similar organization less than a year earlier. Not feminists, but religious fanatics. There was just something all too strange about four boats exploding in the same area where SELF had established its Ten Thousand Islands retreat. Maybe there was a connection, maybe there wasn't—but I wanted to find out more before our welcome was worn out. When people tie up with a cause—any damn cause—the first thing they forfeit is their desire to relate to others outside their cause. Whether the cause is right or wrong, human understanding becomes a casualty. And without understanding, people can get dangerous. Damn dangerous.

I gave Saxan Benton the most disarming smile I could muster.

"Look," I said, "you'll have to forgive us both, Saxan. Westy there is one of my best friends, and like me he's all for women's rights—is that true?"

"Ah, it's true, it's true," O'Davis joined in in his heavy Irish brogue.

"But we still slip into the stereotype from time to time." I shrugged. "Like I said—we're sorry. It's just that we're impressed with what you've done here, that's all. Forgiven?"

She looked at me for a long moment, the awkward fierceness draining from her face. Obviously, it was an uncomfortable role for her—that of the female militant. She cleared her throat. "Yes, of course you're forgiven. And please understand why I was so short with you. It's just that the little things become such irritants. And we've worked so very, very hard here."

"I can see that, Saxan."

She glanced around the office. Overhead, a ceiling fan labored with the heavy June heat. Outside, you could hear occasional laughter reminiscent of a girls'-school playground. "It is beautiful here, isn't it?"

"Aye, it is, it is."

Saxan smiled wanly. "I wish I could say that I had masterminded the whole project, but that wouldn't be true." She seemed as happy as we were to change the subject. She talked on about the goals of her organization and the island itself. She had been hired by SELF four years earlier to teach practical botany at the organization's various outpost schools—and she had given up an assistant professorship to do it.

"Basically, SELF is a temporary haven," she said. "There's a lot of bad that can happen to a woman in the outside world. Our goal is to provide an organization where women in trouble—any kind and any degree of trouble—can go for help. With us, they can reeducate themselves, or rekindle their interests. Or just plain rest."

"It sounds like a worthwhile cause, Saxan."

She made a little church with her hands, then opened them: *see all the people.* "I think so. As I said, there are a lot of bad things that can happen to a woman."

"Like Barbara?"

She sighed wearily. "God, how awful that must have been. The very idea of being trapped on a boat with those . . . those animals."

She shook herself.

"But Barbara seems to already be handling it pretty well—thanks, apparently, to some of the classes she's taken here."

Saxan Benton nodded. But she didn't have time to reply. Through the laughter and summer quiet of the island came a distant piercing scream. A woman's scream; nothing playful about it. Without hesitating, the beautiful woman with the auburn hair was on her feet and running.

And the Irishman and I were right behind.

It was a woman all right.

One of the nude ones we had seen on the way in.

Saxan went curving this way and that along the shell paths across the island. Other women were on the run, too—all hurrying toward the source of the screams. She ran well. Surprisingly well. Usually, women run with the awkward swinging of hips and shoulders that mark the untrained athlete.

But not this woman. It was all I could do to keep up with her, all three of us running dead out, the Irishman lagging slightly behind with his stocky bulk.

"The beach!" she yelled. "The screams are coming from the beach!"

Caught in a flashing still life, I saw that her perfect face was pale, and her autumn-hued hair swung across the small of her back in disarray.

For the first time I saw what she must have looked like as a little girl—frail and troubled.

"Any idea who it might be?"

"Those bastards . . . if it's those bastards again . . ." And she left the rest unfinished, saying little but implying much.

They were net fishermen. Four of them. The oldest looked to be in his mid-twenties. He had greasy black hair and a couple days' growth of beard. His white T-shirt had turned brown with sweat stain and lack of washing. He wore soiled jeans and white rubber fishing boots, and there was a suggestion of a tattoo beneath the black thatch of forearm hair. The other three were similarly dressed but younger. They stood shoulder to shoulder on the beach, laughing drunkenly while their tattooed leader played tough guy with the girl who had been sunbathing.

It was the one with the Polynesian black hair we had seen on the way in. Hers was the oriental face of the islands. Long oiled hair, dark hips and breasts. Tattoo had her by the elbow, trying to make her dance with him. She alternately slapped at him and tried to cover herself with her free hand.

"Come on now, bitch!"

The girl gave a ferocious jerk, pulled away, and took only three steps before one of the others stuck his foot out and tripped her. She fell heavily in the sand, fat hips and thighs jiggling when she landed.

"Stop that immediately!" Saxan Benton didn't even slow down. She was hell-bent on making the rescue her own way—until I grabbed her.

"Damn it, hold on! O'Davis and I will take care of those guys."

She whirled on me. "Don't do that again—don't touch me again! And we don't need your help!"

It was like an echo of something Barbara had told me aboard *Sniper*: "We can take care of ourselves just fine."

And then I saw what they meant. From behind us, on the path, a half-dozen women with billyclubs came running towards us. Their hair hung from beneath the white riot helmets they wore. A couple of them still wore bikinis from swimming, and the others wore cutoff jeans. Holstered on thick gunbelts were cans of mace. When they reached the beach, they immediately stopped running and began to march in tight formation toward the four fishermen.

Stupidly, the men began to laugh and taunt when they saw the women coming. Their plastic face masks were up, and there was no mistaking what each and every one of the women had in mind.

"Sweet Jesus," said Westy. He stood beside me, hands on hips, breathing heavily.

"Looks like it could be messy," I agreed.

"Brother MacMorgan, I notice that yer takin' a dip of yer fine strong Copenhagen. Does that mean what I think it means?"

I motioned toward Saxan Benton. "She told me to stay out of it."

"But I'm a-thinkin' that certain people on the beach there are in serious danger of dyin', Yank."

I returned the tin of spent Copenhagen to my shirt pocket, feeling the good burn of the snuff upon my lip. "The women?"

"Hah!" he snorted. "The men, you thick-headed snit!"

"Just testing you, O'Davis. Let's go—and you take the two guys wearing knives."

"Yer a wonderful friend, Mr. Dusky Mac-Morgan."

Against Saxan's wild protestation, the two of us went trotting past Mahogany Key's version of a riot squad. The fishermen weren't prepared for a man-to-man confrontation, and it subdued them momentarily. With their attention diverted, I noticed that the Polynesian girl had finally scampered to safety. One of the other women wrapped her in a towel, and she buried her face in her palms, crying softly.

"Hey there now, boys, you two ain't involved in this!" Tattoo had retreated just enough at our approach so that he stood at the edge of the water with his three greasy friends. None of them was particularly big. Tattoo was right at six feet, 180 pounds, maybe. The others weren't as big, but they all had that dirty look; that attitude of mean-ness which implies a background of bar fights and knifings.

I noticed that they all reached for their knives now.

I stopped about six feet from Tattoo. O'Davis was an imposing hulk right beside me. "Why don't you fellows just jump in your two mullet skiffs there and get the hell off this island before you get hurt?"

Tattoo had his folding knife in his left hand, palming it. "An' just who in the hell is gonna make us, buddy boy?"

I made myself chuckle, rolling the snuff in my lip. "I got a feeling those women behind us got plans of making little tiny grease spots of you boys."

"*Shit.*"

He drawled it out, using the impact of the word to cover the short steps he was taking toward me. I knew what he had planned: get in a good overhand shot with the knife, and then help his friends handle the Irishman. These were Everglades fishermen, boys who had grown to manhood living the roughest and dirtiest of lives. Fighting was a way of life for them—and they played for keeps.

"Unless you want to learn to say grace through your asshole, you'd better stow that knife, kid."

"*Shit . . .*"

The knife came up in a round overhand arc toward my face. But I was ready for it. I hit him with a glob of amber spittle right in the eyes, then easily ducked under the knife when the acid impact of the snuff temporarily blinded him.

"Goddamn, man!" He bent away from me, clawing at his eyes. It was too good a target. Just couldn't pass it up. I gave him the best my right Topsider had to offer, smack in the butt. It sent him wheeling through the shallows, head down, until he collided unexpectedly with the big wooden mullet skiff he had anchored there. There was an impressive *thunk*, and Tattoo collapsed in the water face up, a thin trickle of blood oozing from his forehead.

I had hoped that the ease with which I handled their leader would scare the other three off. But it didn't. The first of them came charging at me like an old feral boar, case knife held low. I was ready for him, had my moves planned—when two of the riot squad women stepped in front of me. At the last moment, they stepped away from his charge in the way a matador would turn away from a bull, then both clubbed him solidly behind the head. It is a sickening sound, that moist *whack* of wood against bone, and I noticed in the instant that it didn't even seem to bother them. The two women stood there and watched him melt into the sand, holding his head in agony. They were both big women—tall, rawboned, but amply endowed with female accouterments. •

"Take that, you bastard!"

I was about to say something when the last two fishermen made their charge. They hit the two women from behind, driving them down to the ground. They got in a couple of good kidney punches before I finally pulled them off. From the corner of my eye, I could see the other members of the enforcer squad moving into position. But I didn't want them to help. I don't like to be anywhere near when billyclubs are being swung.

The first guy I pulled off was quick. And damn tough. He twisted suddenly to the left, then came back hard with his right elbow and caught me full in the nose. To the ears of the victim, the sound of cartilage exploding is unmistakable. Blood shot down across my blue shirt, and my eyes watered so badly that I could barely see. He hit me chin-high with two quick rights, and I caught the third on the rebound. I folded his arm behind him, busted a couple of ribs with one short left, then hit him hard beneath the ear with a full fist. He went down in my blood patch in the sand and didn't stir.

The last of them no longer liked the odds. He was a greasy little blond guy with a nose like a letter opener. He backed away from me, hands fending me off.

"Hey, I'm convinced, buddy, I'm convinced."

"Then tell you what, you little twerp—stick these lunchmeat friends of yours in those skiffs. Then you walk back here real nice and polite and apologize to these women."

"I didn't even touch them—"

"Move!"

So he moved. And then came back nice and polite, made his apologies to a hundred or so stony female faces, then roared off—turning only to give us that universal one-fingered sign of contempt when he was safely away.

O'Davis came up beside me. My eyes were still watering, and I could barely distinguish his face.

"Ye seem to be bleedin', brother MacMorgan."

"Astute, O'Davis. You're a shrewd one."

"Is it that yer face is now crooked, or could it be that yer fine Scottish nose has been mashed?"

"A broken nose will just give me more character."

"Ah, that's true. An' I understand that certain fat ladies react very kindly ta a nose like that one. Appeals to their maternal instincts—or so I hear."

"O'Davis?"   .

"Aye, Yank?"

"Do you want to tell me now why you let me fight those three guys by myself—or do you want to surprise me later?"

"Well, it's like this, ya see. Now didn't ya say meself was to take the two with knives? Aye, ye did. Well now, they *all* had knives. So I jest decided to be polite an' take the ones ye dinna want. Frankly, Yank, I feel ye were a bit hoggish."

"You're a wonderful friend—Mr. Westy O'Davis."

"Ah, 'tis true. An' keep yer head back, Yank— yer leakin' turrible."

I felt a warm hand touch my shoulder, and then another press some tissue into my hands.

"Are you all right, Dusky?"

It was Saxan Benton.

"My friend here says that I've suddenly become rather ugly. Other than that, I'm just fine."

I was surprised by the tone her voice took, and by the way she squeezed my arm. "And I couldn't disagree with your friend more."

"Were any of your . . . women hurt?"

"I don't think so—but they're going to the infirmary for a checkup. And so are you, by the way."

"No, I think we'll just get back on my boat."

"I'll not hear another word about it."

"Saxan, it's really not necessary—"

"Not another word!"

8

She came to my bed that night.

I didn't know who it was at first.

But it didn't take me long to find out.

We had allowed ourselves to be talked into spending the night. I wanted to stay and get a better reading on these women of Mahogany Key. But like the island's director, Saxan Benton, no summary statements were to be had. For a while everything would check out; all facts and personalities fitting into neat little categories. But then some small thing would happen, or I would come across an indecipherable look, or some stray fact, and my tidy presumptions would crack like old china.

The Irishman wanted to stay for obvious—and maybe better—reasons. As he put it: "Dusky, me boy, we've been invited to spend the evening on this fine tropical island. Now, need I remind you, this is not jest any tropical island. This island is inhabited by five score and more of the finest-lookin' ladies a poor Irish lad like meself could ever hope fer. An' do ye realize, brother MacMorgan, that in certain courts of law in this fine land, we could be committed ta various mental institutes fer refusin'!"

"I'm not sure I believe that, O'Davis."

"Well, if it 'tis not true, Yank, it *should* be."

So we stayed.

Saxan Benton had walked me to the infirmary, leading me by the arm. My face hurt like hell, and with the adrenaline still drugging its way through my brain, it was tough to be civil.

"I guess I should be thanking you," she had said.

"Another Kleenex would do just as well."

"But I did tell you that we could handle it."

I pulled my arm away. "I guess I should have just let those goons beat your two enforcer-squad girls to death when they had them on the ground, huh?"

"They're not girls!"

"Well, they sure as hell fought like it."

"For your information, all six of them are martial-arts experts!"

"Maybe they ought to wear signs—scare the local fishermen away."

She took my arm again, trying to shake me.

"You can be so fine and sincere sometimes, and then turn right around and be a regular ass—why is that?"

"I'm acting like an ass, huh?"

"Yes!"

"Hmm . . . I guess you're right, Saxan. I guess that means we finally have something in common, huh?"

She could have exploded. But she didn't. I sniffed and cleared my eyes enough to see the look of stern authority melt from her face. And then the laughter came, fringed with a certain shyness. She found me looking down into her eyes, and quickly averted them the way a child with crossed eyes might.

"I'm funny, huh?"

"Yes. And you're a mess. Here's the infirmary—and I think you'll like your nurse. It's Barbara."

While Barbara worked on me, Westy went for a walk—said there was much of the island he hadn't seen. She tittered at that. The other women in the small clapboard infirmary gave indifferent looks. It was a small room with cot and stainless-steel instruments, and it smelled of alcohol and balsam shampoo.

"So how are you feeling, Barbara?" Her nurse's uniform consisted of shorts and a striped blouse with buttons that strained against the weight of their two charges. She had showered and scrubbed her tan face pink, and she smelled of soap.

"Oh, a hell of a lot better."

"Where did you learn to swear like that?"

She looked at me for a moment, and when she was sure I wasn't condemning her, she smiled and said, "I guess I do swear a lot, huh? Maybe it's because I never did as a kid. And my overgrown husband—hold that tape right there for a sec, huh?—my husband didn't think it was ladylike. The bastard." She chuckled again as if enjoying the simple freedom of profanity. "I guess you know your nose is broken, huh?"

"Crossed my mind. How crooked is it going to be?"

"Well—here, before I tape it solid, let me show you." She walked across the room, the firmness of her making the wooden floor creak. She got a steel surgical mirror and came back toward me, polishing it on her shirttail. For the first time, oddly, I noticed that her legs—compact and well formed—weren't shaved. She stopped before the table where I sat. "Hey, before we do anything else, let's get rid of that shirt. You're going to stain the floors."

I stood up, stripped off the shirt, and turned to face her, wadding it up in a ball. I'm never ready for the wide-eyed look and the sudden intake of breath when a woman sees me for the first time with my shirt off. I'd like to think it was my physique—but I know better. One long-gone night off the coast of Coronado while I was in SEAL training a big misplaced dusky shark tried to make a meal of me. I lived—barely. The shark didn't. And

I came out of the attack with a new nickname and 148 stitches that left a full-moon scar that starts at my abdomen and circles down across my pelvis.

"Jesus H. Christ!" she whispered.

"Mind if I just throw this shirt in that trash basket?"

"What in the hell happened to you!"

"I won second prize in a shark fight. What about the shirt?"

"The trash basket, yeah. Son of a bitch. . . ."

I took the mirror and held it in front of me. Same blond hair—a little shaggier than I like it. Same heavy jaw that seemed too weighty as a kid and cursed me with an occasional slight stutter. Same blue-gray eyes, same undistinguished ears, same two front upper teeth slightly chipped and never fixed, same glassy scar on the right cheek— a present from a guy with a knife who later became a friend. A dead friend. Everything the same, sun-lined from long days on the sea. Everything unchanged except for the nose. The young fisherman's elbow had chiseled a hump midway up it that would have done credit to an Apache. And it had been pushed a little to the right. The knife scar gave it symmetry.

"I guess it's not too bad, huh?"

"Shit, are you kidding? That's the most unbelievable scar I've ever seen."

I lifted her chin up with my finger. "My nose, woman. You're the doctor, remember?"

So she went back to work with gauze and tape, trying her best to pull my face straight again.

And while she worked, she talked. She had gone to see her Zen instructor immediately after getting back to the island, and was now even more convinced that what had happened aboard the *Blind Luck* made absolutely no difference. I was impressed with her resolve. And happy for her, too. But I am afflicted with one of the common devils: suspicion. Face value isn't good enough. If a genie materialized from a bottle, I'd blow my first two wishes getting background information. So I found myself using the confidence of this new girl to pry out data. Great guy, Dusky MacMorgan. I come across an island full of women content to live—and perhaps love—without men, and I immediately make them prime suspects in the destruction of four drug-runner boats. And what the hell do I care about drugrunners? In my three assignments from Stormin' Norman Fizer, I had gone through a couple of dozen of them with the same regard a machete has for a hothouse tomato. Had I met the actual terrorists at a CIA dinner party—if they have such things—I probably would have congratulated them. So why the concern? For me, it was a rhetorical question. I know why: I'm fascinated by question marks; I'm driven to solve great unsolvables. That's why I've never allowed myself to work a crossword or jigsaw puzzle. I know that if I finished just one, I'd be hooked for the rest of my life. And short of cards, I can't think of more useless wastes of time.

"This Mahogany Key really is something, Barbara. I'll tell you, I'm nothing but impressed."

"Isn't it great!" She smiled as if I had complimented her on her beauty. "And that Saxan—she's just the finest person alive, I think."

"I've only known her a couple of hours, but I see what you mean. Beautiful women aren't supposed to be smart—that's the old stereotype, isn't it?"

"Right!" She shook her head while she ripped off more surgical tape. "The things that woman has done. She's a pretty famous botanist, but I bet you didn't know that. Had some kind of Yukon plant that she discovered named after her. You know, like in Latin or something. And then she was a top cover girl for a couple of years—I'm sure you saw her. You know, she was on the cover of every magazine there is. Then she was a college professor, and then she got interested in the feminist movement, and joined up with SELF. And she's only in her early thirties!"

"Amazing," I said, honestly impressed. "Barbara, maybe I shouldn't ask, but I've wondered. She really is beautiful, like you say, but . . ."

"Her eyes," she said quickly. "That's what you're wondering about, right? I wondered, too. I mean, you have to look hard to notice they're off center. And I guess it actually helped her career as a cover girl. They said it made her look exotic or something. But you still have to wonder why someone with her background didn't have them fixed."

"So why didn't she?"

She shrugged. "I don't know. Saxan's a wonderful person—but she's real private in her own way. Like with the plants: you can be talking to her, and all of a sudden she'll see some plant and, wham, she's in her own little world. She's never talked to me about her eyes. And we're . . . pretty close. I figure if she doesn't want to talk about it, it's her business." She leaned over me, breasts warm against my forearm, tongue clenched between her teeth, concentrating. "Hold still now, I'm almost finished."

"So Saxan is pretty much responsible for the whole complex here, huh?"

"Well, more than she'd probably let on. I guess the newest big backer, though, is some older woman who lives up the coast a ways. On Sanibel? Yeah, Sanibel. I've met her. She was here about a week ago. She's one of those women who wears great big floppy hats and wigs and fights for causes. Her name's Abhner—yeah, that's it. In the last year, she's become pretty much a recluse or something. Sun's ruined her skin, so she can't go out. So Saxan runs the place."

I had been trying to think of a way to get one last bit of information out of her, and decided there was really no completely tactful way. So I did the best I could.

"Barbara, you really have been nice to us. You and Saxan especially. Wes and I are going to be vacationing in the area for another week or so, and I was just wondering . . . if you have the time, maybe you and Saxan would like to be our guests aboard some evening for dinner? I don't have much in the way of good wine, but the fighting deck is fine for dancing, and we could guarantee fresh fish."

It was like I had injected her with a sudden case of the jitters. She dropped the tape she was holding, and banged her head on the table when she stooped to get it. It told me all I wanted to know. And the disappointment I felt was genuine. It seemed like such a terrible, terrible waste.

"If Saxan's engaged with a guy or something— or you are—I'd certainly understand."

"Oh no, nothing like that. It's . . . well, thanks for the invitation. But we don't get off the island much. You know, too busy." She tried to make a joke of it. "Remember, we came down here to get away from men."

I tried to ignore the uncertainty in her bright-green eyes.

"And you and the other women actually don't miss us?"

She patched one more chunk of tape across my nose, stepped back, and admired her handiwork. "All done," she said.

I chuckled, still making a joke of it. "You didn't

answer my question, Barbara—you don't miss us men?"

She let her breath out slowly, then smiled. "Sometimes," she said. "Yeah, sometimes I do."

It was one of those grotesque chunks of bad theater I imagine they've redirected a thousand times in the porno flicks. Not that I'm a connoisseur of skin films. I'm not. They fill me with a sense of the pathetic. They make me feel like some unsuspecting vagrant watching amoebas writhing beneath a microscope.

But mostly they just bore me.

But this was not theater.

After my nose had been bandaged, Saxan made it a special point to invite us to stay for dinner. I was surprised. But pleased. She seemed to feel as if she owed us something; something that went beyond a dinner. I didn't know what.

But there was something about Saxan Benton that fascinated me. Maybe it was because she was quite possibly a lesbian. If so, it was a weird fascination.

Anyway, I agreed to stay—on one condition: that they let Westy and me provide enough fish for at least a chowder.

"Wonderful," she had said, that same delicate look of uncertainty in her blue, blue eyes. "It's funny, but with all this water around, we still can't seem to catch many fish."

"Maybe you need some lessons?"

She grinned at that. "Maybe. We'll talk about it at dinner."

So Westy and I went back to the *Sniper*, went over our gear, tied some new leaders so they would be ready when we wanted, then fired up the little Whaler.

Coming in, I had noticed that the southern end of Mahogany Key was shoaled with a long chunk of oyster bar that jutted off into the channel, then curved around along the other side of the island.

It looked like ideal snook country. The snook is one of Florida's top game fish. It has a long anvil-shaped jaw that sweeps back into a projectile body, complete with a black lateral racing stripe. It's a wonderful fighter, and even better in the kitchen.

So we decided that it was snook we were after. And, if that didn't pan out, we'd head outside to the grassy flats off Panther Key and fish for seatrout. They would be good enough for a chowder.

I jumped the little skiff onto the plane, cutting across the shoal waters at the shoulders of the twisting channel.

"I figure we can anchor above the bar, past that point, then wade down on the inside of the bar if nothing happens."

"An' why not jest wade the bar, Yank? Not that I mind gettin' me feet wet."

"Kills the oysters. Too much wading can ruin a bar. Does that seem silly?"

"Not atall, not atall. I say, kill what needs killin', and protect them that doesn't."

Twenty yards from the point of the bar where the green water funneled off toward deeper water, I shut the Whaler down and drifted until we were close enough to anchor. The Irishman was casting a big, rattling artificial lure, popping it slowly across the surface through the eddy water. We'd had luck on jigs earlier, so I bounced a small yellow bucktail over the bottom along the edge of the bar. I had on a new Quick reel loaded with three hundred yards of twelve-pound-test Stren line, and three feet of forty-pound-test mono leader. The books tell you to use wire leader for snook because their gill plates are like razors. And they're right— you won't lose nearly as many fish with wire leader. But you also won't get nearly as many strikes.

Westy came up hard on the first fish: it hit with a *whoofing* explosion right by the boat, made a sizzling run for the mangroves, then did a tail-walking jump and threw the lure.

"Mush-a-mush!"

"Such language!"

"Did ye see the size o' that bloody monster! Musta been a thirty-pounder!"

"Fish usually look smaller at a distance, O'Davis—those are some eyes you have."

"Well, at least twenty pounds then!" he said indignantly.

"Fifteen pounds is generous—but it was still a big fish. Try setting the hook next time."

He sniffed and fumed and braised me with malevolent glares, then started casting again.

We took two good snook in the next twenty minutes, then stepped out of the Whaler and waded down on the inside of the bar when ladyfish came in and chased us off the point. A ladyfish puts up a fine fight on light tackle, but when it gets to the point where you can't cast without hooking one, it's time to move. Besides, they ruin themselves on treble hooks and I hate to see them die without reason.

So we slogged our way down the bar, casting out into deeper water. We moved as quietly as we could, saying nothing so as not to spook the fish.

We saw the women when we came around the point: two of the long-legged ones who had worn the enforcer squad helmets earlier. They were lying on a blanket beneath an amber gumbo-limbo tree. They were naked and intertwined in a passionate tangle of arms and legs and breasts and buttocks. The smaller of them had long blond hair; the other, close-cropped brown hair.

It was an awkward moment, to say the least. There we stood, up to our thighs in muck and water, while behind us the two women writhed in love-agony. O'Davis gave me a sidelong glance and a "What should we do now?" shrug. I motioned toward the bar. Oysters or not, we were taking the easiest way back. The Irishman actually tiptoed: a ludicrous sight with a spinning rod in his left hand and a twelve-pound snook in his right.

We got back into the skiff, said nothing, then

powered on back to *Sniper*. It was nearing dusk. The sun threw a bronze glare across the Gulf horizon, turning the mangrove line of Hog Key and White Horse Key into a thin black hedgerow. A dozen white ibis flew in low formation toward their roosts, passing over with an arid *whoosh*. On Mahogany Key, the frame buildings caught the last of the sunlight, glowing white and singular among the rush of shadows. I noticed that the big pontoon boat that had been docked ahead of *Sniper* was gone.

"Do ye want a beer, lad?"

"You have to ask?"

The big Irishman lumbered across the deck and came back with a brace of Tuborgs. He sat in the port fighting chair beside me, and we both swiveled back and forth pulling at the beer, feet braced on the transom.

"Some island, huh?"

"Aye. I feel like a cat that's jest watched two birds fight to the death. Sorta cheated, ya know."

"You can't condemn them."

"I mean, it's nice ta see that someone's coverin' all the sexual options, Yank—but sech beautiful women! Nary enough of them to go around as it is."

"Only if you're a glutton."

"Oh, I am, I am. And I'm beginnin' to think this is a strange place fer the likes o' us ta be after all."

"Maybe stranger than you think, Westy."

He eyed me for a moment, then gulped the last

of his beer. "Now, ya wouldn't be meanin' that fine figure of a woman Saxan Benton, would ye?"

I shrugged. "Maybe. Maybe Barbara, too. Maybe all of them. Hell, I don't know. Normally, I'd just write it off as their own private affair, and leave and forget it. But that business about the drugrunners keeps nagging at me—hey, get another beer for me too, okay?"

So we sat there in the last of a fine June day and talked about it. O'Davis had his suspicions, too. Fact: four drug boats had been destroyed in less than a year. Fact: all of them had gone down off the Ten Thousand Islands. Probability: someone local, someone with a good cover, was involved.

"But why would these women do sech a thing, Yank?"

"Damned if I know. Maybe they're in the drug business themselves and don't like competition. Maybe they just don't like drugrunners. Or maybe they just don't like men. Or maybe they have absolutely nothing at all to do with it."

There was a wry expression on the Irishman's face. "Keep in mind that at least one of us is a classic figure of manhood—an' yer rather masculine-lookin' yerself, MacMorgan. Discountin' the napkin taped ta yer ugly nose, o' course."

"Of course."

"An' if it's true they've got a passionate hatred fer men, we might be in serious danger, eh?"

"May not live through the night."

The Irishman sniffed, wiped his face with one big red paw. He still held the wry smile. "I kin see that ye want to abandon our holiday to pursue this matter. Do ya have any immediate plans, me American friend? Or is dyin' in yer sleep good enough for ye?"

"I thought we might visit my hermit friend on Dismal Key tomorrow. He keeps a pretty close eye on what goes on around these islands. And maybe we'll head up toward Sanibel Island."

"Another little vacation?"

"Yeah—that, and the woman who backs this organization supposedly lives up there. I guess it wouldn't hurt to poke around a little. Maybe even call a friend or two up in Washington."

The enforcer-squad girls, done with their business, walked the water's edge, past the docks, and up the Indian mound toward the big house where Saxan Benton kept her office. They wore short shorts and halter tops, hips wagging away from us. They were holding hands.

"I'm beginning ta feel a little bit like Ulysses, brother MacMorgan."

"I know what you mean: women on the cliffs calling us poor mariners to our destruction. You know, they're dangerous, but they're so pretty it doesn't matter."

The Irishman watched the two women disappear into the clapboard house, a wistful expression on his face. "Lovely they are," he agreed. "Homeric."

9

Dinner at the Mahogany Key Center of SELF was not what I had thought it would be.

I expected a communal dining hall with loud laughter and the clatter of plates.

Instead, the women cooked in their cabin and ate alone or with friends.

As Saxan Benton explained, "We're together all day anyway. So why eat together? Besides, we really don't have the facilities to cook for a hundred and twenty-five women. And the last thing someone wants to do when she comes here is kitchen duty for someone else."

So Westy and I ate with Saxan in her room. Just the three of us. Nice and cozy. While Saxan and I sat over drinks on the porch of her little cabin, the Irishman broiled one of the snook on a tiny gas stove. He was a volunteer. A happy volunteer. He likes to cook almost as much as he likes to sing—and that's saying something. And besides, there had been an unspoken understanding that I had taken a special interest in her.

So he cooked. And we talked.

It was a nice little cabin: one bedroom, a stone fireplace for blustery nights, ceiling fans, hanging plants, watercolor seascapes, and a wall of books beside a window that looked out across the island. I looked at some of the books, then gave up. All complex biology and botany, containing words I could barely pronounce—let alone understand.

"You write any of these?"

She stood by the doorway, a frosted glass lipped with a green sliver of lime in her hand. She wore navy-blue cotton slacks, a soft gray blouse and sandals. Her hair was piled in soft folds atop her head. She looked feminine—yet businesslike. Beautiful—yet unapproachable. The way she moved, the way she held her head, the way she looked at you all added to the paradox. She was the loveliest of enigmas. And maybe that's why I felt that adolescent ache deep in my abdomen when I was near her. She would give a little of herself with a touch, a laugh, or a smile, only to jerk it away and close the doors behind. It wasn't indifference. And it wasn't teasing. There was an essence of confidence about her, but it was cored with vulnerability.

Whatever it was, I was infatuated with it.

And her.

"You asked if I wrote any of those." She gave

a little deprecating laugh. "I wish I had. The only thing I've ever had published was my master's thesis. And it was hardly a best seller."

"Barbara says you tend to be too modest."

"She said that? What a nice thing to say. But it's not true. The fact is, I'm not very interesting."

"You seem pretty interesting to me."

She turned away and, boom, the doors closed. We went out to the porch and sat in wicker chairs side by side. But not too close. She fiddled with her drink. For a moment, the conversation was strained. Outside, birds gawked and squawked from their nocturnal roosts. Mosquitoes whined to get in through the screening. The haunting wood-wind notes of a mangrove cuckoo wafted through the night air. The full moon frosted the island in silver.

"I noticed that the pontoon boat was gone when we got back from fishing."

"What? Oh. Some of the women went into town for a few things. Fuel, mostly. We use a lot of it out here. Way too much, really. We get it in Everglades City."

"I hope they don't run into those four goons who were out here today."

She sipped at her drink. "Oh, the townspeople don't give us any trouble. I assume those men are staying on an island near here. A bunch of them do off and on. They sleep and drink during the day, then fish illegally at night. Occasionally they give us trouble. You know that commercial fishing has been outlawed in the National Park, don't you?"

"I do. But actually, we're not quite inside the boundaries."

"Which is exactly why they camp near us." She gave a little shiver. "I wish someone would do something about them. They . . . they're horrible."

"You didn't seem frightened today."

She looked pleased. "I didn't? Good. I don't like the other women to see me frightened. But those men do scare me. I keep planning to turn them in, but I never have. This is such a desolate area, there's no telling what they might do."

"Maybe blow up some boats?"

She looked at me strangely. "Now why would you say that?"

"Someone's doing it. The Coast Guard has a special crew out trying to find exactly who and why."

"I know," she said.

"You do?"

"Barbara told me." She shifted slightly in her chair, that peculiar look of vulnerability showing on her moonlit face. "Do you mind if I ask you something? Barbara also said that the Coast Guard was going to arrest you. But then suddenly decided not to."

"That's right. They had overlooked a few bits of information, and I just filled them in. No lawman likes to be charged with false arrest. That's all there was to it."

She hesitated for a moment. "For some reason, she got the idea you were more than just an average innocent citizen."

"Yeah?"

"She said the Coast Guard officer—what was his name?"

"Chief Spears?"

"Yes, that's it. She said he treated you like a fellow officer after you had talked to him. Those were her exact words, by the way: 'fellow officer.' "

"She's all wrong—but why the interest?"

Saxan seemed a little embarrassed. Her face flushed, which made her eyes look even bluer. "Did it seem as if I was pressing? I'm sorry if I was. But the way you handled those men this morning, and that scar on your face and side . . ."

"Barbara told you about that too, huh?"

"Oh, God, now I do sound like a snoop. What I mean is that you obviously have some familiarity with violence, that's all." She looked at me a long time, as if studying my face. "It's just that, for some odd reason, I find you . . . you . . ."

"You find me what, Saxan?" I touched the tape on my nose. "Grotesque?"

Hers was a fine deep laugh. "No. It's strange, but I find you . . . well, anything but grotesque. Do you ever get that feeling about people—as if you know everything about someone, but really know nothing at all?"

"Funny you should mention it, but I met a woman like that this morning." I held her eyes for a moment: strangely haunting and haunted off-center eyes.

And then her private door slammed again.

Bang.

The guy who jumped me was Tattoo—the one I had kicked headlong into the skiff that morning. I guess he decided he had to come back for a little revenge. At first I was surprised he hadn't brought some help.

And then I realized he had.

Our dinner was one of the Irishman's finer efforts. He had sluiced the broiled snook in melted garlic butter, and served it with fresh lime. With it were fried island-grown plantains, and fresh fruit salad from their little citrus grove. We had brought cold beer with us, and Saxan nursed another gin and tonic. The conversation was pleasant and superficial, but even so, it told me more than I had known about the woman's background. She had been the wealthy daughter of a man she obviously didn't care to talk about. She had traveled extensively, moved in the right circles, attended the best schools. There was no mention of a marriage, no mention of a man ever having been in her life. And I wondered all the more about her interest in me—if she was, indeed, interested.

Afterward, Saxan and I went out for a walk. Westy insisted that, since he had cooked, he should clean up. The look he gave me told me that I owed him another favor: the first for saving my life in Cuba, the second for giving me some time alone with this woman.

"Now, you two folks jest go on outside an' enjoy the moonlight. It's a fine soft night, it is, an' I won't be long with the dishes."

Moonlight suggests romance. And the mention of it seemed to make her nervous. She kept her hands stuffed into her pants pockets as we ambled down the Indian mound toward the water. She stopped once and gently fingered the shriveled leaf on one of the jasmine trees as if she suffered with it.

"Nice bush, jasmine."

"Hmm . . . doesn't it smell wonderful, Dusky. Are you interested in plants?"

"About the same way I'm interested in cats."

"That's a funny way of saying it."

"They go their way and I go mine."

"Oh."

"You can't afford to be fascinated by everything. It spreads you a little too thin."

"I suppose so."

I stopped and took her hand. "But I am fascinated by you."

She looked up into my face. "Don't, Dusky. There's something about me you don't understand."

"I understand that this morning you told me never to touch you again. But now you're not pulling your hand away."

She made a halfhearted effort to remove her hand, then let it stay. "Let's walk," she said.

It was down by the docks that Tattoo jumped me. A few seconds later I understood why. He didn't want me to get near *Sniper.*

I was about to say something clever to Saxan; you know, something designed to make her chuckle. But I never got it out. Suddenly there was this dark figure swinging down out of a chunky wisp of oak tree. In the strangeness of that moment, I thought: Geezus, they got gorillas on this island.

But it was Tattoo.

He came swinging down and hit me flush on the head. The blow staggered me. It sent me wheeling backward, fighting to clear the cobwebs. Little red and green lights popped off and on in my head. My nose burned.

There was a scream.

"You stupid bastard!"

I heard the fleshy *smack* of knuckles against flesh, the rustle of bushes, and then Saxan was standing over me.

"Hey, are you okay, Dusky?"

I had landed butt first on the shell path, like someone who is having a bad time with roller skates.

I pulled myself quickly to my feet. "What in the hell happened?"

"It was one of them; one of the men from this morning. He jumped out of a tree on top of you."

"Only one?" I shook my head, trying to chase the fog away. I noticed that my nose was seeping again. And that Saxan was massaging her right hand, as if she had hurt it. "What happened to you? Are you hurt?"

I took her hand in mine. It was already beginning to swell. She looked more shocked than I. "I guess . . . he was coming at you again, and I . . . I just hit him in the face as hard as I could with my fist." Her giggle was close to tears. "I've never done anything like that before."

"Thanks, kid."

"I hit him really hard. He looked so damned surprised." She studied her hand for a moment. "It's throbbing—but it doesn't hurt at all."

"Give it time," I said. "Did you see which way he went?"

She didn't have time to answer. They had doused *Sniper* with gasoline. Luckily, they hadn't had time to do a thorough job. There was a two-cylinder roar of a small outboard, and then as I strained to see them through the moonlight, a hollow *whoosh* as my sportfisherman ignited.

"Saxan, stay here! Get O'Davis—quick!"

I sprinted down the docks, feeling the heavy planking sag beneath my 215 pounds. It looked like the end of *Sniper*. The entire wheelhouse was in flames. It was like seeing a favorite horse on fire, and I half expected her to scream. But she just sat there in the calm June night, stolid and sure. And burning.

In long strides I half ran, half jumped from the gunnel to the top of the cabin, then grabbed the lowest stainless brace of the flybridge and pulled myself up to the deck, where the upper controls are located. But I had no intentions of starting her up. The big 2A40BC fire extinguisher was bracketed beside the pilot chair, where I knew it would be. I ripped it free, pulled the pin, turned, and made one long jump down onto the fighting deck.

The flames were still fueling themselves on the gasoline. The gas can they had used was capless, sitting in one of the fighting chairs. In one swift motion, I swung it overboard, then turned the extinguisher toward the base of the flames.

Its hoary spew smothered them with a harsh *hoosh.*

I gave it a moment, smelling the acrid stink of burned plastic and gas, then emptied the rest of the extinguisher on the last remaining embers.

"I brought the weenies, brother MacMorgan. Where's the fire?"

O'Davis stood on the dock, broad arms on hips, his red beard looking black in the moonlight. He wasn't smiling.

"The assholes," I said.

I could feel the adrenaline pouring through me, cold and deadly.

"Damage?"

"Melted some of the ignition wires, ruined the pilot chair. The cabin stinks like hell."

O'Davis hummed a troubled snatch of an Irish

tune. "Might be a fine night ta pay a visit on yer playful friends. Pretty moon, it is—an' I haven't beaten anyone daft in too long."

"Not tonight," I said.

"Is this a new side of yerself I'm seein', lad?"

"Not tonight," I said again. "They'd be expecting us."

I was lying. I didn't care if they were expecting me or not. And I didn't care on which island they were camping, how near or how far. The fact was, if I found them tonight, I would kill them. I know that coldness that comes over me all too well. And you just don't go around killing rowdy fisherman.

No matter how much they might deserve it.

"Tomorrow night," I said. "We'll speak with them tomorrow night."

"Aye, then tomorrow it is." He stood watching me for a long moment, and then: "An' the more I study the look on yer big ugly face, Yank, the wiser that decision seems."

"Don't you have some dishes to do?"

"No. But I did meet a young woman here. Student o' folk songs, she is. I've promised ta sing to her—and her friend, o' course."

I looked up at him and forced a smile. He winked back.

"Of course," I said.

Saxan was waiting for me on the end of the dock. She was still rubbing her hand.

"How's your boat? Is it badly damaged?"

"Yeah. Fire will do that."

"Well, you don't have to get mad at me!"

I whirled on her. "Saxan, you may think this island is the best thing since seedless grapes, but since I've come in contact with it, I've almost been arrested, and had my nose broken and my boat vandalized. Now, forgive me if I seem a little upset, but it's just that this is beginning to seem more and more like a bad roller-coaster ride. Just as things start falling into place, the whole puzzle collapses and I end up getting smacked in the face. Now, damn it, Saxan, something stinks around here. I don't know what it is, but . . ." I caught myself just in time. "I don't know and I don't really care. If we can borrow your Shamrock tomorrow, I'll run into Everglades City and get the necessary parts for my boat. Then we'll let you women get back to whatever it is you do on this island."

I got that sense of emptiness from her again, as if she had shrunk back into a hole: some tiny, blue-eyed creature peering out at the rest of the world.

"I'm sorry," I said. "That last part was cruel."

"It doesn't matter."

"It does to me."

She shuddered slightly. "There's nothing going on here, Dusky."

"If you say so."

"These women are all good people. They've all

been injured in one way or another, and although they might seem wicked in the eyes of the rest of the world . . ."

"I don't want to hear this. . . ."

"Maybe it's because we frighten you."

"Maybe you do."

Jasmine bushes bordered each side of the dock. They were in heavy bloom, making the June night sweet with their odor. I reached over and broke off a big cluster of the small flowers.

"Here," I said. "Physicians wear stethoscopes. Botanists ought to wear flowers behind their ear."

She cupped the jasmine in both hands, hiding her face in it.

"Dusky?" she said.

"Yeah."

"Your nose is bleeding again."

"I know. With any luck, the creep knocked it straight this time."

10

I was asleep in the infirmary when she came to me.

Barbara had done a new plaster job on my nose, and stuck a bucket of ice beside my bed.

Saxan had insisted that I stay ashore. And she was right. Until I got *Sniper* scrubbed and aired out she really wasn't inhabitable.

"I'm becoming a real pro at fixing mashed faces," Barbara had said gaily. She had changed into long jeans, and she wore some kind of white, loosely woven blouse that was all but see-through. The dark-brown symmetry of areolas stood out invitingly and the material clung to the contours of her breasts.

"One more time, and I'll need a transfusion."

She had laughed. "Maybe you need one now. Damn, if you aren't looking pale. And you're kind of trembling."

She was bending over me, breasts warm against my shoulder, brushing my face occasionally. A ceiling fan whirled beneath the white globe of infirmary light, and it gave Barbara's short blond hair a celestial glow.

"I think your shirt's ruined again."

"Looks like I'm going to have to make another visit to Sears."

"Goddamn, you have broad shoulders. Like a weight lifter or something."

"I grew up in the circus. Worked the trapeze."

She stood back and looked at her handiwork. "Circus, huh? Jesus, what a kidder you are. And you still look pale. You feeling okay?"

"It might have something to do with that shirt you're wearing."

She looked down at herself, as if surprised. "What? Oh shit, I didn't realize. Look, I'm sorry if it bothers you."

"Don't apologize."

She looked uncertain for a moment, then pleased. "Hey, that's kind of nice. You're affected, huh?"

"I think I can give you a solid yes on that. Why so surprised?"

She shrugged. "It's just that my ex-husband had a way of making me feel like a pile of shit about this high. Ugly, you know. And those bastards on the *Blind Luck* didn't help any. This is the first time in a long while I even thought about being . . ."

"Attractive?"

"Yeah." She smiled. "That's a nice way to put it." She took a deep breath and let it out. "So—Saxan says you're to sleep right here. And that you can use our boat tomorrow to go into town."

"Too bad this didn't happen earlier—I could have caught a ride in on the pontoon boat."

She looked puzzled. "What?"

"Saxan said some of the women went into Everglades City for fuel."

"That's odd. That town closes up tight as a drum at six. Maybe they just had to make some phone calls or something. All we've got out here is a CB radio—and that doesn't work half the time. Saxan's trying to scour up enough money now to get a VHF with a big tower—in case of emergencies, you know. She's going to talk to Ms. Abhner about it."

There was an awkward, sensual moment before she finally turned to go. Then she stopped and turned back.

"I don't want you to take this the wrong way."

"Take what the wrong way?"

She came over to me on the table, leaned down slowly, bright-green eyes looking into mine, and kissed me. She drew back, then kissed me again: her lips warm and moist and open.

"Nice," she said softly.

"Is that part of the prescription, nurse?"

"Kind of," she said softly. "For one of us."

She flipped the light off, shut the door behind her, and was gone.

*   *   *

It was almost three in the morning when Saxan came to me. I know because I checked the green glow of my Rolex when I heard the infirmary door open.

She stood there in the pale moonlight for a long time, undecided. She wore some kind of gauzy, hip-length T-shirt. I could see the silhouette of her body firm and taut, nipples elongated in the upward thrust of breasts. Twice she retreated outside, but then stepped back.

"You're letting mosquitoes in."

She jumped, startled.

"You're awake?"

"I'm not sure. It's a nice dream if I'm not."

She stood in the moonlight and said nothing.

"Come over here. We can talk about it."

"No," she said.

She turned her back to me, and I thought she was leaving. Instead, she stripped the T-shirt up over her head in one smooth motion and let it drop to the floor. She had nothing on underneath.

"No," she said again. "Let's not talk. Not now."

She came gliding through the soft light and shadows, her skin luminescent in the night. I lay motionless as she kissed me twice experimentally. She trembled, then pulled her lips hard down on mine, the violence of it sudden and surprising. My left hand moved up the curve of her buttocks and found her breast, firm and swollen.

She jerked back. "Don't," she said. "Please . . .

just let me try on my own. Please, Dusky. Can you lie still?"

"I can't speak for all of me," I said softly.

I heard her move away, heard her fumble with something on a shelf, and then the sound of a radio: strings and timpani, music loud and bold on a tender night. She came back and cradled my head against her chest, stroking my hair.

"I'm frightened."

"I know."

"Maybe I should just leave right now."

"Maybe."

"You don't care?"

"I care very much. But it's your decision."

She stayed for nearly an hour. It seemed like five minutes. She was like a blind child seeing a new room for the first time with her hands. She was gentle and unsure, kissing and exploring with lips and soft fingertips.

"Is that . . . nice?"

"Very."

"And this?"

"Nicer."

Only once, much later, did she let herself give in; let me pull her to me in a passionate joining of lips, allow my hands to trace her body, to feel her warm and open and ready. And just as suddenly, she jerked away.

"No, Dusky, please . . . I can't."

"I think we both know that's not true."

"No, I can't."

"Then that's enough for me."

I felt her relax, smile. "You don't look as though it's been nearly enough."

I took her hand and kissed it softly. "Believe me, whatever you want is enough for me."

"I can't see how you can say that."

"I can say that because I mean it."

She got up and pulled the T-shirt down over her head, giving me one last moonlit-look at firm breasts, flat stomach, and the silken curl of pubic hair shadowing down into thighs.

She came back and kissed me gently on the forehead. "Do I love you?"

"That's a tough one, Saxan."

She reached up and switched off the radio. "Yes," she said. "It certainly is."

In the morning I got up, stretched, pulled on my cotton khaki fishing pants, threw my shirt away as a complete loss, then studied the swollen mess of gauze and tape that was my nose in the mirror.

Self-evaluation: "You'll never make it in the movies with an ugly map like that, MacMorgan."

I headed out the door, then stopped. Someone had brought up one of my extra shirts from *Sniper*: one of the short-sleeved blue ones that had been washed and worn until it was almost gray. I slid it on and read the little note:

"Don't want that scar to shock the other women. Thanks for the medicine. Barbara."

Dr. MacMorgan, always ready with a little medicinal affection. It made me feel sort of silly.

O'Davis was down at the water's edge putting on a casting demonstration, lecturing a half-dozen women in his best Irish brogue. Across from him, in a little clearing among the gumbo-limbos, a couple dozen other women formed a circle, making their own karate *dojo*. Within the ring, two women in rubber pads and helmets were putting on a demonstration in full-contact karate.

At least I assumed it was a demonstration. The way they went at it, it looked like a death match.

I recognized them both from Mahogany Key's small squad of enforcers. One was a stocky brunette with hams for legs. The other was the tall woman with the short brown hair Westy and I had stumbled upon while fishing. She was striking enough with her clothes off. In the whirling flourish of full-combat karate, she was awesome.

For all you hear about it, you rarely come across an honest to God natural-born athlete. But this lioness with the close-cropped hair was one. You had only to watch her move, to know it. There was no awkwardness, no wasted effort. As a dancer, she would have been unbelievable. As a martial-arts expert, she was devastating.

The stocky girl held up well for a while, doing her best to stay inside, fighting it out with short jabs and shin stabs. But then the lioness took control, driving her kicks home with more and more certainty. The stocky one's face was flushed, and her breathing came in labored, nasal *whoofs* that were the beginning of her defeat. Finally, she went down in a heap after a straight right hand to the head—not so much from the force of the blow, but because she knew it was time to throw in the towel.

The tall one helped her to her feet. They embraced, then bowed. The tall one put her hands on her hips, barely puffing, and surveyed the audience. For some reason, her eyes caught on mine.

"Want to try it?"

She had a husky voice, slightly abrasive. I felt all eyes turn and lock on me.

"I'd better not." Actually, I did want to try it. Some demon of masculinity deep inside wanted me to prove the final physical superiority: combat.

"Afraid I'll hurt you?" She disguised it as an offhand, joking remark, but there was an edge to it. A couple of women in the circle laughed nervously. The rest looked on steely-eyed.

I pointed to my nose. "I'm already hurt."

"Convenient," she said.

I heard her snicker as I turned and walked away.

O'Davis was just finishing his casting demonstration. I waited while he went through a couple of basic fishing knots—recommending the uniknot for general purposes—then walked with him down to the docks.

"Aren't we lookin' chipper this fine mornin', lad."

"I slept well. By the way, where did you stay?"

His elfin eyes glinted. "Until England gives us our wee isle back, all the world's home to an Irishman."

"How you do go on."

"Me folk-singing friend offered me her billet for the night. It woulda been ignoble of me ta refuse, bein' a fellow artist an' all."

"I see."

He offered no details, and I asked for none. For all his grandiose ways, Westy O'Davis was not one of those men who feels obligated to go into graphic detail about his sexual exploits. I admired that.

"I figure it'll take us about an hour here to get *Sniper* cleaned up, and then we can jump in the Shamrock and pick up some wire and parts in Everglades City. Maybe stop and see my hermit friend at Dismal Key on the way."

"An' tonight?"

"Tonight I'd like to track down my tattooed friend and give him a few lessons in maritime courtesy—namely, you don't go around setting other people's boats on fire."

"Sounds delightful."

"And if you see that I get carried away and try to choke him to death, please pull me off. I don't like jails."

"Oh, I will, Yank, I will—after a decent interval, o' course. You need yer recreation, too."

We borrowed mops and buckets and went to

work on *Sniper*. There was some smoke damage, and some melted wires, but other than that she was in fine shape. I was lucky Saxan and I had gone for our after-dinner walk.

We were just about finished when Saxan came down to see me. She was brisk and businesslike—no sign of the woman who had come to me the night before. I noticed that she watched O'Davis for some bawdy exchange; some secretive look between us that would be evidence I had told all. When she saw none, she seemed to relax a little bit.

"It certainly looks better," she said.

"Once I get the parts I need, it'll take me about twenty minutes to get her going. Of course, I'll have to replace the pilot chair."

"Oh, that's too bad."

She wore one of those terry-cloth tennis suits. The colors brought out her eyes. She wore her long auburn hair in braids. It made her look nineteen.

"I guess you'll be busy all day, huh?"

She meaningfully held up the clipboard she carried. "I'm afraid so. I have a stack of these evaluation sheets to finish. And I've got some interviews to do. The term ends in two days."

"And then what?"

"Some of the staff will stay around. But most of the women will go home—I hope, as more self-reliant people."

"And you?"

"I'll stay."

"Good," I said. "Maybe we can get short-and-ugly here to cook for us again."

She smiled a distant, noncommittal smile. "That would be nice."

After assuring Saxan we would take loving care of SELF's handsome Shamrock, Westy and I idled away from the docks. The 302 Ford engine burpled prettily.

"Nice boat."

"Aye—an' a wonderful name, too."

I craned to study the docks momentarily.

"Say, Westy—you were up before me, right?"

"Aye. Me folk-singer friend wanted ta sing before sunrise."

"Did you notice the pontoon boat coming in?"

He thought for a moment. "No. It was back when I got up."

"And it wasn't back when those goons set *Sniper* on fire. And that was an hour after dark—about nine-thirty or ten."

"Hmm. The ladies musta come home real late."

"Yeah," I said, thinking. "Very late. Westy, at about three a.m., what were you and your folk-singer friend doing?"

"Yank, the impropriety of yer question offends me."

"Were you singing?"

"Aye, ya could say that, yes indeed. But why?"

"Just want to make sure you're getting enough practice in. That's all."

11

Tattoo and his seedy friends were camped on the southeastern bank of Panther Key.

They had set up their tents among the palm trees and Australian pines in the same clearing where the legendary hermit Juan Gomez had lived and, supposedly, kept a cache of pirate treasure buried beneath the floor of his shack.

The shack and the gold—if they ever existed—were long since gone: just the remnants of a foundation left.

There were about a dozen of them. More than I thought there would be. They had their overpowered mullet skiffs tethered well offshore because of the strong spring tides. They sat in a big screened-in picnic tent drinking and laughing and telling graphic stories and jokes.

When I heard the owl call—hoarse Irish lilt and

all—I knew that we were ready. I also knew they wouldn't be laughing for long.

Earlier in the day we had motored the little Shamrock along the outskirts of the Ten Thousand Islands, past Round Key and Tiger Key, and then picked up the well-marked channel into Everglades City.

It was a Saturday, and there were a few other boats out: private fishermen mostly, sticking to the channels so they wouldn't get lost in the bowels of that wilderness.

I hadn't been to Everglades City in more than two years. In fact, it was the last real trip we had made before my wife, Janet, was murdered. And pulling into the mouth of the Barron River, past the graceful white clapboard Sunset Lodge, and then approaching the early-1900s elegance of the Rod and Gun Club, a wave of nostalgia hit me.

Everglades City is an ideal place for nostalgia. It looks like a little New England village built, strangely, between the Everglades and the Ten Thousand Islands back country. Time has eroded its population, gave and then took away a bank and a courthouse, but it has not burdened the village with that concrete-poured-to-form malignancy the modern builders call "progress."

Its sturdy wooden houses, yards perfectly kept, lifted themselves on pilings at the water's edge, and the old globular streetlights still dotted the tree-lined avenues.

"Ah, lovely, Yank, jest lovely. I kin see by yer face that this is a special place."

"It was," I said simply.

"Yer wife's special place?"

"Yes."

I saw the dark sadness that seemed always just beyond the Irishman's eyes come to the forefront. It made his bearded face solemn and prophet-like.

"Me wife an' I had sech a place too. A wee bit of a cottage on Cayman's west end called Frank's Sound. I canna bear to go there now. I know how ye feel, Yank."

It was the first time he had ever mentioned having a wife. And the pain it caused him was evidence why.

There are some things a man just doesn't want to talk about.

I said nothing.

I pulled the Shamrock up to the gas docks of the grand brick-and-clapboard Rod and Gun Club with its striped awnings, its palms, and long screened-in dining porch. There was an air of permanency about the place; an atmosphere of back-country elegance. An old man came shuffling up, wheezing with some kind of respiratory problem. I told him to top off the tank of the Shamrock, and handed up the near-empty six-gallon can for the Whaler we had left behind.

"Can we leave our boat here while we have lunch and do some shopping?"

"Certainly, sir."

"Would you know if they might have some stone crab left over from the season?"

"I'm not sure, sir. But we just got some fine pompano in."

We walked across the lawn of the Rod and Gun Club and along the empty summer streets to the town's little general store. Two little blond boys in T-shirts and jeans sat outside on the steps, their upper lips purple with grape Nehi. The store had the few things I needed—minus the pilot's chair, of course. I paid the nice lady and exchanged comments on the weather, and we walked back out into the gathering June heat.

A stray setter went trotting by, and the smell of jasmine was heavy in the morning air. The juxtaposition of the two made me think, strangely, of Saxan. I wondered what she was doing at that moment; pictured her going over her reports, the core of vulnerability now well buried on that island without men. She had gotten to me. I couldn't deny that—especially to myself. What had she said?: *"Have you ever felt as if you know everything about someone, but really don't know him at all?"*

It was as if she had spoken my own innermost thoughts.

About her.

We strolled down the middle of the empty streets, past the little playground, to General Telephone's sterile and incongruous transmission outpost. For this blight, the village received in return a brace of pay phones. The first person I called was Norm Fizer in Washington, my own private link to the federal bureaucracy.

He said that the wife and kids were fine, and that D.C. was sweltering and, no, he hadn't done any fishing. The pleasantries thus out of the way, I asked him the few things I wanted to know.

"Boats exploding?" He seemed surprised. "I may have heard something about it—but the Coast Guard is handling that, right? And by the way, what in the hell was that business about them arresting you? I had half a mind to let them haul you away."

"It's a long story, Stormin' Norm. I appreciated your help, though."

"So why the interest in these boats? Are you desperate for another assignment? Because, if you are . . ."

"Hey, I'm on vacation, remember? Just a little natural curiosity, that's all. Say, can you have your computers check out some people for me?"

Westy was listening while I talked. He seemed especially surprised at one of the names I gave Fizer. After I had thanked Norm and promised to call him back in a day or two, I hung up. Westy was giving me a quizzical look.

"Brother MacMorgan, you dunna possibly think that . . ."

"Some things just don't add up, Westy. It can't hurt to check out everybody."

I borrowed some more change from the Irishman and turned to the phone again. Barbara had said that SELF's newest benefactor lived on Sanibel Island. Sanibel is one of the more popular vacation spots on Florida's west coast because of its shells, and because the condominium maniacs haven't been allowed to build their highrises any damn way they want—yet. The Florida builder has to possess one of the strangest of mentalities. He gauges his success by the sheer mass of excretions he drops within the communal nest; gleefully weighing his bankbook against the architectural putrescences with which he inexorably transforms and finally destroys his own homeland.

They really are a strange breed. And Sanibel is one of the few places in Florida where they have been even slightly restrained.

So I called a friend of mine on that crustacean-shaped island: Mack Hamby, who runs Tarpon Bay Marina there. Mack is an amazing guy. He gave up a top position in a massive banking corporation to spend his days dealing with the things he enjoys: shells, boats, fishing, and a select band of raving independents and humorists he employs.

Mack collects paintings of clowns for his house. And he gives jobs to those who have never been painted.

Mack is always trying to hire me.

"MacMorgan! Have you finally gotten smart and decided to come and guide out of Tarpon Bay?"

"Can't, Mack. Business is too good in Key West."

"You're always worrying about the little things, Dusky. It's only money." He chuckled sagaciously. Being an honest to God financial wizard, Mack likes to joke about money.

"Look, Mack, I need some help."

"Tarpon Bay is open three hundred and sixty-five days a year just to serve, Dusky. What's up?"

'There's a woman up there named Abhner. She's supposed to be kind of a feminist."

"MacMorgan, my interest in feminists began to smolder when those ladies stopped burning their bras. Besides, my beautiful wife says I'm a hopeless chauvinist."

"And Eleanor is right as always. Look, Mack, this woman is supposed to be pretty active in causes. I'm told she wears lots of big hats and flowing dresses. I want to find out what I can about her. Have you ever seen her?"

The other end of the line went silent for a moment. I could hear Mack questioning people in the background. Finally, he returned.

"Nope. I haven't, and no one here has heard of her. But George says there's a man on the island by that name. Willie says he's a commercial fisherman."

"A guy, huh?"

"Yeah. In his mid-forties—right, George?"

I heard George agree in the background. "But there's no woman on the island by that name?"

"Hell, Dusky, there probably is. I don't know everyone here anymore. Place gets more crowded every year. But give me a day or two, and I'll find out."

"I'll check back with you in a day or two, Mack."

"Are you on your way up?"

"Probably. Be there in a few days, probably."

"Good. By the way, you owe me money, MacMorgan."

"For what?"

"For this custom-made tarpon rod I'm going to give you an unbelievable deal on, that's what. Just bring a blank check. I'll fill in the figures."

"I'll mail it first thing in the morning, Mack. I can hardly wait."

We walked on back to the Rod and Gun Club and took plush chairs in the screened dining area beside the stump of the big Madeira mahogany. The waitress was a pretty Everglades City high school student, and she blushed when Westy chided her for bringing glasses with our beer orders. "Beer glasses are for old ladies, me dear!"

I went with the old man's advice and had the pompano—which was excellent—and the Irishman had one of the thick cheeseburgers with a slab of sweet onion, and the potato salad.

It was not a meal for conversation. The pompano came with a side order of garlic toast, and baked potato with sour cream, and I spent the better part of a half hour doing it justice.

When the meal was finished, the Irishman took out his long cherrywood pipe, tapped the bowl full of some sweet cavendish, and sat back, utterly relaxed.

"Nice place, huh?"

"Aye, it is, it is."

"Did you get enough to eat?"

"It's an odd mother ye make—why the concern, Yank?"

"Just want you to have plenty of energy for tonight."

He grinned.

The bar of the Gun Club was plush and dark, and it took my eyes a while to adjust when I went in for more beer. There was a huge mounted tarpon, yellow with age, above the clerk's desk, and beyond that the full skin of a twelve-foot 'gator. There were only a few people at the bar. A stocky man in a Coast Guard uniform caught my eye— and then I knew why.

"Hey—Chief Spears?"

He eyed me for a moment, and then his face lit with recognition. "MacMorgan? Well, I'll be damned."

He still had the stub of cigar jammed between his teeth, and he wore his duty whites, complete with service medals. He shook hands as if genuinely glad to see me.

"Have a beer with us out on the porch?"

He stuffed out his cigar in one of the large ash-trays. "I'll have a Coke with you out on the porch. I had to give up the other stuff five years ago."

"The same time you gave up snuff?"

He laughed. "Yeah—but I think I miss the snuff more."

I grabbed a couple of paper cups from the bartender and cradled fresh beers in my left hand, and we went back to the porch. Chief Spears sat down squat and bulky next to the Irishman.

"Ye wouldn't have abandoned yer own ship now, would you, Chief?"

"Just like an Irishman to think the worst. Right, MacMorgan?" We all laughed. Spears took the tin of Copenhagen I offered him gratefully and settled down with the paper-cup spittoon. "No," he said. "Like I told you, the *Royal Palm* isn't my ship. I just do duty on her to . . ." He hesitated, then started on a new tack. "You know, when I got chewed out for arresting you two, I got the impression that the higher-ups have a lofty regard for your knowledge in this kind of work."

It wasn't a statement. It was a question. He wanted to know if he was free to talk shop with us.

"We know how to keep our mouths shut, if that's what you mean."

"Good," he said. "In that case, I only do sea duty when I'm working on a particular investigation."

"Like boats being blown up in the middle of nowhere?"

He nodded. "Lately, it's been that. But I'm kind of a troubleshooter. It's what happens when you're too old for sea duty, and too mean for a desk. When the other fellas have trouble, they send me out to have a look." He spit expertly into his cup, then glanced up at me. He had wide dark eyes, bushy black eyebrows, and a face that suggested he had done his share of brawling in other days, other wars. "By the way, MacMorgan, what happened to your beezer?"

I told him about our stop on Mahogany Key, and about the goon who had cracked my face. I didn't mention the fire aboard *Sniper*. I didn't want to give Spears any reasons for getting to them first. I had a feeling he wouldn't leave much for me.

"I know the guys you're talking about," he said, nodding his head. "Every one of them was born for the state pen. Or . . . maybe the federal pen."

He said the last meaningfully. "You mean you think they're mixed up with the drug boats that've been going up? But why?"

"MacMorgan, tell me and you can have my job, stripes, plush office, and all." He spit again and took another sip of his Coke. "That's why I took a couple of days ashore. You know, talk to the locals, see if they have any ideas. In a small town like this, word gets around."

"Any luck?"

"No. The crew you're talking about isn't local. Apparently they're from down in the Keys someplace. The locals hate them. They're camping out on Panther Key, and they give them a wide berth. Word is they came up here to fish the National Park illegally."

"So why don't you get the marine patrol boys to haul them in? Get them for breaking federal laws, then check them out on the other at your leisure?"

"Because I'm not sure." He stopped for a moment, thinking. "You said you spent a little time on Mahogany Key with those women's libbers, right?"

"Yeah."

"You know they're mostly homosexual, don't you? Lesbians?"

For some reason, I found his words offensive, but not his tone. It was cold and professional.

"We suspected it." I said nothing more. I was interested to see if he had the same suspicions about the women there as I.

"I talked to the dockmaster up at the marina. He says they run their pontoon boat back and forth between here and there at all sorts of strange times. It kind of nags at me. Why would lesbians come into a small town like this for their fun? And you can't get supplies here at night."

"Mebbe lookin' for a little friendly conversion?" O'Davis suggested.

Spears chuckled. "I wouldn't bet my firstborn

on it—and being in the Coast Guard, that's about all I'd have to bet. The problem with checking out Mahogany Key is how to do it without them getting suspicious."

"I'd like to help, but we didn't leave under the best of terms."

"I can imagine," he said. When he got up to go, he turned back and smiled. "Hey, about that breezer of yours, MacMorgan."

"Yeah?"

"Don't be too tough on those guys. I've got enough investigations underway as it is."

We stopped in to see my hermit friend, Al Seely, on the way back.

Al lives every harried man's secret dream. A dozen years ago, when he was still in his forties, he got fed up with the big city and the life he was living, canned it all, and found the remotest island he could to set up camp. Now he lives in a peeling frame house on an Indian mound on one of the wildest, loveliest islands around: Dismal Key.

Believe me, there's nothing dismal about it.

He came down to his narrow plank dock when I pulled the Shamrock in and snubbed her off. He wore the same black Injun Joe hat as always, complete with osprey feather on the broad brim. He had his pipe clenched between his teeth and a smile on his broad face, and his little black dog, Digger, barked at his heels.

"Doggone, look what the cat drug in! You

haven't been here in so long, MacMorgan, I thought you'd finally sunk that big boat of yours!"

He insisted we come up to the house with him and set a spell. Al lives simply, but well. He's a damn competent artist, and he keeps his oil paintings displayed all over the living room, so visitors can enjoy them when they come. Along with that, he does some writing, reads everything he can about the history of the Ten Thousand Islands, and, when there's nothing else to do, cuts new paths through the island's jungle.

He's one of the few men I know brave enough to live exactly the way he wants to live.

When we had taken our seats, and Al had told me everything new there was to tell about the island, I explained to him why we had stopped.

"Mind if we anchor in the little cove off the houseboat tonight, Al?"

"You know I don't mind. But why don't you just stay up here with me? You know I've got plenty of room."

"We will, Al. But not tonight."

He looked at me shrewdly. "This wouldn't have anything to do with those twerps camping up on Panther Key, would it?"

"Do you know *everything* that's going on in these islands?"

He grinned. "Like Thoreau says: You've got to slow down if you want to see the world speed by. That plus the fact I know they've been raising Cain all over the place. Came up here and gave me a hard time once. Heard you'd had some problems, too."

"I don't want to bring any trouble in on you, Al."

"Oh, heck, Dusky, it's been too quiet around here lately anyway. You bring in all the trouble you want, any time you want. I'm not afraid of those hoodlums." Al has a nice wild laugh, like Andy Devine's, or John D. MacDonald's. He gave us a burst of it, and loaded up his pipe. "But why don't you just go ahead and confess the real reason you're here?"

It surprised me. "What?"

He laughed again. "That's the real reason you're up in these parts, you old pirate," he said, pointing out the window. And, sure enough, he was right again. It was a school of big tarpon moving through the deepwater channel off Dismal Key. They sparkled silver in the late June sunlight, rolling: big fish, up to 140 pounds.

"Al," I said, "you should drop this hermit business and go into mind-reading. You'd make a bundle."

He chuckled. "But only with people as easy to read as you, MacMorgan."

12

The girls on the beach didn't even bother walking to cover at our approach this time.

Maybe it was because they recognized their own boat.

Or maybe it was because they recognized us.

They lay there oiled and naked, baking in the sun. One of them was the brown-haired amazon. She had one long leg bent, the other outstretched. Her arms were folded lazily above her head, and her face was turned to one side. The pose lengthened her and added an upward thrust to her heavy breasts. She was a striking picture indeed.

O'Davis hazarded a friendly wave. The other women pretended not to notice. The amazon gave him a frozen stare.

"What happened to that charm you're always talking about, Westy?"

He shook his head sadly. "Ah, the poor lass—

tryin' so hard to pretend like she's not attracted to me."

"Heck of an actress, if you ask me."

I kept watching for Saxan while we worked aboard *Sniper*. Every time I got up for tools, or more cold beer, I would scan the expanse of the island. But it was business as usual on Mahogany Key. Women went back and forth between the white clapboard buildings. And in the little clearing where I had watched the full-contact karate, a tawny-haired beauty in a black leotard led thirty other women in yoga exercises.

But no Saxan Benton.

"Now, who would ye be lookin' fer, Yank?" O'Davis asked me wryly.

"What? Oh, no one. Just taking in the scenery, you know."

"It wouldn't be that fine-lookin' director, would it now?"

"Saxan? Of course not."

He chuckled. "It's a bad liar ye are, brother MacMorgan. Have I told ya that?"

"Not unless you count every day since I first met you."

It took longer than I thought to get the ignition system rewired. Repair work on a boat always takes longer than you think it will. Naval architects build them as if every marine mechanic were a midget with gorilla arms.

But I finally got the last wire crimped in, folded the jumble back up under the wheel casing with the help of a tie-wrap, then helped the Irishman clean up the mess.

"Well," I said, "might as well try 'er."

I turned the key and punched in the ignition buttons, and *Sniper* roared to life, the twin 453 GMC diesels rumbling prettily.

"Sounds great, doesn't she?"

"Fer a bloody stinkpot, she doesn't sound too bad, now."

I punched him lightly on the shoulder and wiped my face off with the towel he offered. "O'Davis, you haven't said a nice thing about powerboats since Castro's boy confiscated that big windship of yours down in Mariel."

"Aye, I admit it! But I'll get 'er back—jest ye wait an' see, Mr. Dusky MacMorgan."

I looked levelly into his craggy Irish face. "Damn, O'Davis—you're not kidding, are you?"

"No. An' when the time comes, lad, you'll be goin' with me back to Mr. Castro's island to lend a hand. Don't be forgettin' that ya still owe me a favor . . ."

"Just a small one for saving my life."

"Aye!"

When we had everything stored away and ready, I went below and showered in the cramped little head. The Irishman eyed me askance, but said nothing. I changed into clean khaki pants and fresh cotton shirt, and actually found myself raking a comb through my hair.

"Say goodbye to 'er for me, Yank," O'Davis said

with a wink. I didn't bother answering. I noticed he was getting cleaned up himself.

It was late in the afternoon; the time of day in Florida when the giant anvil-headed cumulus clouds have taken just about all the thermal assaults they can stand. They drift seaward, purple and swollen, then cast cooled and sweeping veils of rain down upon the land. Every summer's day at four p.m. it happens. You can almost set your watch by it. It rains for about an hour, which softens the air, leaches steam from the asphalt where the city folk dwell, and leaves a hint of something moist and herbal in the sea wind.

Suddenly, it was shower time on Mahogany Key, and I was damn near soaked to the skin by the time I made it up the Indian mound to Saxan's office. Lightning *ker-WHACKED* and rumbled, and the rain rattled down upon the tin roof of the porch. Outside, the women of the yoga class sprinted for cover, trying to protect their hair.

I had to make the screen door bang three times before Saxan finally heard me above the storm. She still wore the neat terry-cloth tennis suit, and her long auburn hair was still in braids. She looked surprised to see me, off-center blue eyes dropping their shield momentarily.

"Came to say goodbye."

"You're leaving? Oh—you're soaking wet."

There was an uneasy silence while I waited for her to invite me in.

She didn't.

"I was just in a meeting."

"Oh."

"I'm . . . it was nice to have met you."

"And you, Ms. Saxan Benton."

She remained on the other side of the screen door, but I noticed her cover-girl composure beginning to fall away. The rain had loosened the tape on my nose. I tried to patch it back in the silence.

"Here—not like that. Let me help, Dusky."

She slid out the door and began tugging and patting pieces of tape. Her fingers were long and warm against my face.

"I'd like to see you again, Saxan."

She said nothing, as if she could not hear me.

"Maybe tomorrow night. I could pick you up about—"

"Dusky, no," she said sharply. She pushed the last bit of tape into place, then stepped back, her blue eyes troubled and defensive. "Do I have to spell it out for you, Dusky? Do I have to come right out and say what I am? You're looking for some cozy little she-partner; someone to share your bed and have a few laughs with, and—"

"The only thing I'm looking for, Saxan, is you," I cut in firmly. "Sure, to share some laughs, but not necessarily to share my bed. But I'd be lying if I said that it hasn't been on my mind all day, because it has. Now if that offends you in some way, I'm sorry. But what I'm mostly looking for is just a chance to spend some time with you, to talk with you—and if that still offends you, then maybe I've been wrong all along, Saxan. As I said last night: it's your decision."

I turned to go, but she caught my arm. Her hand was trembling.

"Dusky, please . . . I'm sorry."

As gently as I could, I reached up and touched each cheek with my hand. "It's nothing to cry about. And it's nothing you have to decide right now. Let's just say you have an open invitation."

"Okay," she said. "Okay."

Her perfect face, tan and soft, was tilted upward toward mine. She seemed hypnotized as my lips neared hers.

"No," she said. But she did not move, her eyes locked into mine.

"No . . ."

She sagged at my touch, then fell into my arms weakly, still trembling. Her mouth was open and ready and wanting, her body alive. She held onto me as if I were a support; the first, perhaps.

With the rain pummeling down upon the tin porch, something so simple as a kiss became a poignant revelation for her; an affirmation for us both—not of a lifetime together, or even, perhaps, months. But an affirmation of willingness.

And then:

"Ms. Benton!"

Saxan whirled away from me, her face suddenly leached of color. A large woman stood in the shadows of the doorway, and I remembered: *"I was in a meeting. . . ."*

It was an older woman, huge and heavy, with a husky masculine voice. Dimly, I could see that she wore thick cake makeup and red lipstick. The massive felt hat on her head was tilted jauntily.

"Oh . . . I'm sorry," she said, her voice strangely edged with fear. Saxan did not have to say the name of the woman for me to know who it must be, but she went on: "I was just saying goodbye to an old friend, Ms. Abhner. . . ."

At midnight, the Irishman and I went over our plans once more, then set out in the Whaler for Panther Key.

I wore my lucky Limey commando knickers, black Navy watch cap, and the only dark long-sleeved shirt I could find. I had my Randall attack-survival knife holstered on my belt, surgical tape in pocket, and thirty feet of good braided line cut into sections.

A late moon cast a yellow haze across the islands, and O'Davis dabbed professionally at his cheeks with the face black in the olive-drab tube. Like me, he wore the darkest clothes he could find—but no cap.

"Yank, no offense," he had said, "but there's a reason why very few great soldiers have been blond. Ye see, once you lose that cap o' yers, yer head glows like a torch. Now, us redheads—

always the best among fightin' men—just naturally blend in with the night."

Having memorized the points and shapes of islands aboard *Sniper* while we cooked dinner and did our planning, I ran the back country toward Panther Key. It was not a difficult route, and the moon was light enough. Besides, I had run it before in other years. I kept glancing off to the south as we skimmed through the twisting channelways and the dark musk of the islands. And then I saw it: the silver expanse of open Gulf edged on either side by islands with beaches that glowed white in the moonlight. One was Hog Key. The other was the island we were seeking: Panther Key.

A hundred yards uptide, I broke the Whaler into idle, then switched her off. It was so calm you could see star-paths in the black water.

"Suppose this means we have to paddle, eh, Yank?"

"Yeah. And keep your voice down."

O'Davis picked up the paddles and fitted them into the oarlocks. He began to push us on toward Panther Key with surprising expertise.

"You smell the smoke?"

"Aye. Campfire. An' I can jest catch bits o' laughter—hear? Yer tattooed friend must be hostin' a party."

"And we're going to provide the entertainment."

We beached the Whaler in the cove on the northwestern edge of the island. The sand was hard, braced with shells, and it echoed with an odd resonance as we walked. Their camp was on the other end of the island, about a mile away. Birds screeched in the trees. Mosquitoes whined, vectoring in, finding us in a gauzy haze.

"When we get to the narrowest part of the island, we cut across, right?"

"Aye. Would there be any rattlers on this island, Yank?"

"Not hardly. Coral snakes kill them all."

"Reassurin'. Most reassurin'."

Tattoo and his friends weren't in any great danger—from us, anyway. I just wanted to get close enough to their camp so that I could listen in for a while. Guys like Tattoo like to drink and brag. And, in his mind, blowing up boats would be something to brag about.

If they were the ones doing it.

And once we had listened for a while, I was going to scare them.

Scare the living hell out of them.

They'd think twice before setting *Sniper* afire again.

The tide was up, and it was tough walking. The beach sloped down sharply with the strong tides of the Ten Thousand Islands, and the higher ground was thick with bayonet plants and sandspurs. We stuck to the beach, keeping a sharp eye on the distant glow of sand.

It was no time to be seen.

When the island narrowed and the voices of the

fishermen were loud enough to cover the sound
of us moving through the bushes, we cut across
the island. Mangrove roots and strangler figs
pulled at our shoes, mosquitoes did their best to
make life miserable, and I was soaking with sweat
by the time we reached their camp.

With a simple hand signal, I told O'Davis which
way he should circle. He went off without a
sound: big broad-shouldered hulk moving from
shadow to shadow with the grace of a cat.

I was sure glad he was on my side.

Picking my footing, I moved in upon the camp.
It was surprisingly orderly. There were six two-
man tents spread away from a large campfire in
a semicircle. Across from the fire was a big
screened-in dining tent. A Coleman lantern hung
from a hook on the main pole brace. It threw its
sterile white light over a makeshift table and
chairs, and on the men within. In one corner was
a box of canned goods. In the other, a stack of
Dacor scuba tanks.

There were about twelve of them in all. It figured. There were six mullet skiffs tethered off the
beach. All of them were equipped with big John-
son 200s mounted forward in an engine box—a
design unique to that particular kind of net fishing boat.

Only, you don't need two-hundred-horsepower
engines to run down mullet. With the boats they
had, they could do forty miles an hour in ten
inches of water. As Chief Spears had said, if the

commercial boys didn't want to be caught, they couldn't be caught. Not by anything short of a chopper, anyway.

They were drinking canned beer from a big red cooler. From the way they were shouting and laughing you knew right away they were really drunk. And a beer-drinking enemy becomes an easy target. You can be sure of that. The more they drink, the more they're going to have to get rid of. And when they move away into the shadows to relieve themselves, that's when you take them. You knock them off one by one.

The dining tent had two zippered doors. When the first of them came outside, I followed him through the shadows to see where it was they went to urinate. The goons sitting on the other side of the table would go the other way—Westy's way.

I didn't take him then. I didn't want to. Not yet, anyway. I just got close enough to check out the spot for an easy attack, then made myself as comfortable as I could and concentrated on listening to the talk inside.

For the most part, it was disappointing. They talked about women, mostly. They told their stories as graphically as possible, each of them waiting anxiously to top the other's story. Tattoo sat at the head of the table. He wore a black T-shirt. He drank beer with his left hand and chain-smoked, his raffish face contorting oddly when he inhaled. They made only minor reference to setting *Sniper* on fire. Tattoo bragged at some length about knocking me on my ass. And just when I was about to give it up and signal O'Davis to start taking them, there was this:

"So, what are you boys gonna do with all this here money we got coming?"

"Shit, man—get drunk."

"Hell, we're already drunk! I'm gonna buy me a boat. A big goddamn boat. Maybe run some shit o' my own."

"What, an' get blown up?"

They all laughed at that.

Tattoo silenced them quickly. "You boys quit talkin' that shit, hear?" He peered out of the lighted boundaries of the tent suspiciously. "Never know who might be out there listenin', man. You stupid bastards gonna end up blowin' the whole scam, bein' blabber-mouthed like that."

"Hell, man—who's gonna hear us out here?"

"Coast Guard, for one thing, fool. Been around here thick as flies lately. An' that one officer stoppin' 'round here askin' questions was just a little too close for comfort, man—what with the shit we got stashed. Didn't like that chief guy, man. Looked a little too savvy."

"Shit, man, you can see that big cutter comin' a mile away."

"He might not be on the cutter, asshole! Now that's enough. No more talk, goddamn it. Not about that, anyway."

So they went back to their jokes and stories. And I knew it was time.

I folded my hands together, blew against my thumbs with the signal we had devised.

The way the Irishman hooted back made me cringe. He sounded like an Irish tenor trying to imitate a television Indian.

But no one in the tent even noticed.

I had no trouble with any of them: neither the first nor the second, third, and fourth. One by one, over a period of a half hour, they all came out to urinate. And I stepped out of the shadows behind them, put the fine Randall knife to their chins, and convinced them that it was in their best interest to cooperate while I tied them and taped their mouths. The dialogue was pretty much the same: "One word, one call, even one loud cough, and I'll stick this knife right through your face. Nod if you understand."

And one by one they understood.

I hoped the Irishman was having equal luck on the other side.

When there were only four of them left, they began to get suspicious. Tattoo was still among them.

"Hey, where'n the hell you think them guys got off to?"

"Checkin' the boats, most likely."

"I dunno. They been gone for a while, man."

For the first time, Tattoo looked concerned. He

got drunkenly to his feet, set his beer down, and yelled, "What you bastards doin' out there?"

His face darkened in the silence.

"They probably just playin' a joke on us, man. You know, tryin' to get us scared or somethin'."

Tattoo cupped his hands around his mouth. "Okay, assholes! You come in here right now and quit screwing around! I'm gonna come out there an' kick your asses!"

I knelt in the shadows, listening, waiting. At my feet, five of his eight missing cronies lay noiselessly, bellies down. Tattoo looked genuinely scared. He turned to his friends. "Hey, you guys, go out an' have a look around. You packin' anything?"

"Goddamn guns are in the boat, man. Told you we shoulda brought 'em in."

"Told me, hell! Just get off your asses an' go find them guys. I swear, I'm gonna slap 'em silly for goin' off like that. Now git! I gotta stay here and guard this place."

The three seedy fishermen went separately into the darkness, working their way around the perimeter of the camp. The first one that came my way had his knife out. I decided not to take any chances. I stood against a big buttonwood tree, and when he came by I hit him with an overhand right, flush on the jaw. He exhaled loudly and went down in a heap. I heard a loud rustle in the bushes on the other side of the camp, and then two similar *thwacks:* the sound of the Irishman's knuckles against jawbone.

Tattoo heard it, too. He lit another cigarette and his hands shook. "Hey, who the hell's out there?"

I let him stew for a moment, and then I stepped out into the clearing of the camp. I saw Westy come through the bushes on the other side.

"Just paying a friendly visit, big man."

He peered through the netting of the tent, and when he recognized me, I saw his face blanch. I started walking toward him.

"Hey, what the hell . . . look, man, I'm sorry we fired your boat, but goddammit it, you gotta learn how to mind your own business."

"I haven't even begun to mind my own business, big man. You're about to get a lesson in how I mind my business."

He fumbled for his case knife and opened it. He had backed into the tent as far as he could go. I slit the screen open with my Randall and stepped through. Westy came through the screening on the other side. Tattoo tried to shrink into his own shadow.

"Look, what the hell you guys want, anyway? Jesus . . . don't looka me like that! What'd you do with my friends?"

"Dead, lad," O'Davis said evenly. Tattoo didn't notice his lips start to crinkle into a smile. The Irishman made a slicing motion, finger against throat. "Cut 'em open, we did."

Tattoo's eyes were wild now, crazy with fear. He still held the little knife, but he knew that it was useless. "You guys . . . you guys are crazy, man!"

"Shouldn't set other folks' boats on fire, kid." I looked at Westy. "What should we do with this vermin?"

He shrugged. " 'Fraid we have ta kill 'im, Yank. Knows a bit too much, wouldn't ye say?"

"No!" Tattoo threw his knife down and, absurdly, put his hands up like a bad guy in a television western. "Look . . . please, don't kill me . . . honest to God, I won't say a word. And I can pay you! I've got money. A bunch o' money!"

That's what I wanted to hear. I was about to ask him where it was; where he had gotten it.

But I never got the chance. That's when I heard the distinctive *click-click* of the double-action revolver, and someone stepped unexpectedly into the tent with us.

It was the woman. She held one of the fine weapons: the Model 60 Smith & Wesson .38 Special. Its two-inch stainless-steel barrel gleamed beneath the Coleman lantern.

"I think it's unnecessary to tell these men anything more, Billy. They know quite enough. As they were telling you—too much. And now we must arrange their deaths."

The heavy cake makeup was still in place, and on the broad-brimmed hat there was now a dark veil pulled down.

It was SELF's benefactor.

It was Ms. Abhner. . . .

13

The amazon woman was no longer a figure of amusement; no longer the symbol of angry feminism to be scoffed at.

She was suddenly stalking me the way a cat stalks a wounded bird.

And there was no mistaking what her eyes held. Her whole face was contorted with hatred.

And death.

She had vowed to kill me; to break me with her own hands.

And now her tongue flickered out, moistening her lips, and her sturdy legs were bent in readiness as she moved toward me through the darkness.

"Try to fight back," she told me. "Please try. . . ."

The Abhner woman was no athlete. She had lumbered behind us, revolver held at ready, forcing us to climb aboard the same Shamrock we had used earlier.

If I had ever doubted a connection between the exploding boats and this strange organization called SELF, I no longer did. And it filled me with a curious queasiness; a queasiness produced not by distaste or fear, but by a disappointment in my gut. It meant Saxan Benton, that intriguing woman, was involved all the way up to her beautiful, strange eyes.

"These two fellows know far too much, Billy," the woman repeated. "And it presents us with a rather sticky problem. They are lawmen—did you know that? No, of course you didn't, you stupid child."

She had a strange, froglike voice. She enunciated her words, biting them off one by one. Tattoo had recovered quickly, converting his earlier fear into a deadly anger. He came over, jerked the Randall knife out of my hand, then cold-cocked me forehead-high.

I forced myself to stay on my feet; to act as if his punch were no more than an insect bite. It infuriated him.

"Goddamn you . . ." He turned to the old woman. "Look, Ms. Abhner, you just give me an hour with these guys. Let me haul 'em offshore in my boat, an' I swear to God they'll never be seen again. I'll cut 'em up into little pieces."

"Stupid, Billy. Very stupid. You see, they have a boat here with them. But of course you would know that, since you set it on fire. By the way, Billy, I was tempted to have you killed for that. Such a stupid thing to do, boy. Their boat is anchored in the cove by Dismal Key, where that pesky hermit lives. The hermit is a light sleeper, you know—misses absolutely nothing. And I'm afraid he would contact the Coast Guard if we tried to just slip away with it. And that Coast Guard officer that's been around here is so very eager to make an arrest. No, we must take them back to the island and lock them up for a time. I think I'll end the term a day early, send the girls home tomorrow. And then we will find a way to get their boat and set up a nasty accident for our friends." She chuckled cryptically. "You see, they must die reasonable deaths, Billy."

It was an odd duo, the seedy young fisherman and this huge old woman. He was afraid of her, no doubt about that. He took her verbal abuse like slaps to the face.

So, she knew that we were associated with a law-enforcement agency. Who had told her? Barbara? Saxan? That was easy enough, but how had she known that *Sniper* was at Dismal Key?

Obviously she had had someone follow us. And whoever it was was damn good.

I looked at the big Irishman. He stood at ease beside me. Tattoo had taken his knife, too. He lifted his eyebrows wryly: a "Well, MacMorgan, here's another fine mess you've gotten us into" look.

"So you and your feminists are getting rich running drugs," I said. "But why bring these goons in on the kill?"

The woman had backed out of the tent into the shadows again. Only her thick hands and the silver revolver caught the light. I heard her click her tongue with disapproval. "You disappoint me, Mr. MacMorgan. I had such glowing reports about your intellect. And now you ask such a stupid question—and at such an inappropriate time. I see no reason to go into it—but I will say that you are totally mistaken in your assumptions."

"If you expect me to believe that—"

"Enough!" She motioned to Tattoo. "Billy, you'll be pleased to learn that your idiot friends are not dead after all. It was just one of Mr. Mac-Morgan's little jokes. I suggest you go outside now and untie them. I suspect you'll have some work to do tomorrow night. Have you refilled your air tanks?"

"Yes, ma'am. Everything's all set."

"Fine. Now, if you'll be good enough to tie their hands behind them—that's right, just as tight as you can get them—I'll take them back to Mahogany Key. One more thing—they had a little Whaler anchored down at the other end of the island. Please find it and hide it. Hide it well, Billy. Or I will make you very, very sorry."

"Right away, Ms. Abhner."

She forced us out of the tent and down the beach. She had run the Shamrock up on the beach, anchoring it off the stern. I kept expecting her to make a mistake; some little slipup that would let me get a good kick in to her chin or neck.

But she never did. She was good. Surprisingly good.

It was nearly three a.m. by the time we got back to Mahogany Key.

The full moon blazed down on the island, throwing silver light and shadows across the buildings and the clearing.

There were no houselights on anywhere. I found myself trying to peer through the darkness into Saxan's little cottage window. I tried to will her to wake up; to confront me. If I was to die, I wanted at least the satisfaction of looking into her eyes to let her know that her apparent hatred for men had had this final triumph; I had trusted her, and for that I would now die.

When we had first approached the island, Westy had compared us to Ulysses, and the island women to the sirens upon the rocks.

If we'd only known then how right he was. . . . .

"If you men would be so kind as to lie on your stomachs while I tie up this boat? That's right— nice and slow. Please don't make me kill you now."

She threw quick clove hitches around the pilings, then came up behind us as she forced us across the Indian mound in the silence of three a.m.

We went past the main house where Saxan's

office was located, then the woman made us lie on our stomachs again while she tapped at the door of one of the cottages. A light flickered on and the screen door swung open. I could turn my head just enough to see the tall woman who had challenged me at the karate demonstration. She stood yawning sleepily in the doorway. She wore only panties and a T-shirt.

"I'm afraid our friends have returned, dear," said the old woman.

The amazon wasn't yawning now. Her eyes sparkled with interest.

"I'll guard them," she said quickly. Her fingers flexed back and forth as she looked at me.

"That's what I was hoping, dear. And Misty, will you please ask your friend to come along and help? I think we'd better separate these two—they're rather big and brutal-looking."

"I've taken bigger," the tall woman said enigmatically.

"I know, Misty, dear. But let's not take chances. And it will only be for another day."

If not for the circumstances, the girl's name would have made me laugh. Misty? It was like calling a killer doberman Spot.

They marched us into the darkness to a part of the island I had never been to before. There was a low squat brick bunker with a cement roof—probably a fresh vegetable cellar from earlier times. Twenty yards to the other side was a larger brick building. From inside I could hear the diesel whoofing of an engine. It was the generator room.

The amazon's friend had come along. It was the stocky blond woman she had fought earlier in the day. Both had changed into jeans and long-sleeved shirts. They smelled heavily of bug spray.

"You brought more rope? Good. Let's put the Irishman in with the generator. That's right, tie his legs well—and check him once more for weapons. These detective types always keep an ace in the hole. And Misty—"

"I know, Ms. Abhner," said the amazon. She came up close beside me, and I noticed absently that we were about the same height. "I'll take good care of him. In the root cellar, right? He won't get away." Her teeth bared into a sickly smile. "But I almost hope he tries. . . ."

So I was in darkness.

The absolute darkness of an ancient brick cellar barely wide enough for me to stretch out in. It smelled of damp earth and sand.

Misty had shoved me in roughly, giving me a well-placed kick in the side after she had tied my legs. She had grunted with pleasure.

"Give me a reason," she had hissed. "Just give me a reason, pig, and I'll take you apart."

"You seem upset about something, lady."

"None of your wisecracks, pig! And don't call me lady!"

"I guess it is a little inappropriate. . . ."

She kicked me again with a force that made the muscles in my thigh knot. "Just keep it up!" And she had gone out then, slamming the door behind.

So think, MacMorgan; think fast and well or you're going to end up one very dead man. What the Abhner woman wants to do is pretty obvious: get you and the Irishman aboard Sniper, *then blow it up. And it's not going to be very long before they get the details worked out. So think, damn it. You've been in tougher spots than this and always gotten away. And you're not going to let these maniac women succeed where the pirates inevitably failed. Right?*

Maybe.

I tried to put myself in Abhner's position. How would I get *Sniper* away without arousing the suspicions of Al Seely? Would they kill him, too? No, too many people knew and liked Al. That would bring down too much heat. It didn't take me long to figure out what the boss lady would do. Keep an eye on Al's shack the next day. And when he jumped in his little skiff to try for a few supper fish, she would have one of her goons snake *Sniper* while she left a note for Al; a note, ostensibly from us, that would thank him and explain why we decided to leave suddenly.

How else could she do it?

So that left us . . . how long? Eight, maybe ten hours? Not very long. No, I had to think of something, and think of something now, before first light.

And I knew that the Irishman was doing the same thing only a few yards away.

Finally, I hit upon it. Not a great idea, but the best I could come up with. I called to the amazon through the thick door. "Hey, Misty! Come in here for a—"

"Shut up, you."

"It's about your friend—the one you were rolling in the bushes with yesterday."

The door suddenly creaked open. She had to bend to poke her head in. She was a looming silhouette backdropped by the moonlit island. "Just what in the hell are you talking about, buster?"

"Hey, don't play coy with me. She told me all about it. We had some fun together last night, and . . ."

She bought it for the briefest of instants.

"Mary Sue? You and Mary Sue . . . ?" And then: "Don't give me that bullshit, buster. But how did you know that we . . . ?"

"Don't believe me, then," I said offhandedly. I was banking on the knowledge that this woman had left her cottage with the stocky blonde, and not the pretty Mary Sue that Westy and I had seen her with. Apparently they didn't share their living quarters, so there was no way the amazon could have known where her friend Mary Sue was the night before. "It's just that we had a pretty good time together last night, and . . . well, since I'm not exactly busy at the moment, I thought you might let her know I'm here." And then I added perversely: "She says you're pretty much the second string, anyway, so . . ."

Jealousy is a particularly vile weapon. It taints both the user and the victim. The words were sour coming out, but I had to use them—and use them convincingly.

And it worked.

I felt the rage within her as she pushed her way into the cellar. She kicked me in the side once, twice; again and again, calling me the liar that I was. When her anger had momentarily subsided, I said, "Pretty brave of you, lady, kicking a man bound hand and foot."

"You pig—"

"You thought the reason I didn't spar with you this afternoon was because I was scared? Well, I *was*—scared I'd hurt you."

That did it. She couldn't get my ropes off fast enough. But, with my hands still tied, she seemed to catch hold of her senses. She stopped suddenly, thought for a moment, then headed back out the door.

"So you are a coward?"

She whirled. "It's just that I don't want to take any chances, pretty boy. Don't worry. I'll be right back. I wouldn't miss this for the world."

I heard her talking animatedly to someone outside—Westy's guard, no doubt. I hadn't counted on that. Would she have a weapon? Probably. It didn't matter. One of them, two of them, it made no difference. It was our only chance.

The stocky blonde held the stainless-steel .38 as

the amazon got my hands untied and shoved me roughly through the doorway. She stood in the shadows, weapon poised and ready. The amazon faced me then, a deadly glimmer in her eye, and I noticed that she reached back and took something out of her pocket. Hands up like a two-armed Buddha, she began to twirl something. And then I knew what: nunchakus, those particularly brutal oriental killing devices of wire and wood. They are both clubs and garrotes, and inevitably deadly in the hands of an expert.

And this woman was an expert.

"Kill him," the stocky blonde said thickly. There was an oddly sensual quality to her voice. "Knock his head off, Misty."

And that's just about exactly what Misty had in mind.

She began stalking me around the little clearing beside the brick root cellar. The nunchakus blazed with perfect symmetry in the moonlight.

"Why are you running, pretty boy? I thought you wanted to fight!"

I kept backing away, palms turned outward as if fending her off. I wanted her to think that I was afraid; wanted her to revel in her self-confidence, because that would give me the time I needed.

"You ready to admit that you're nothing but a dirty lying pig?"

"Believe what you want to believe," I said. "It's not going to change what happened between Mary Sue and me."

"Bastard!"

I was still moving backward, knowing exactly the positioning I needed. I had to take care of the stocky blonde with the .38 before I did anything else.

"Get 'em, Misty—don't let him keep runnin' from you like that!"

"I'll get him, don't worry. It's kind of nice to see pretty boy scared. You are scared, aren't you, pretty boy. . . ."

I had acted oblivious to the blonde, knowing that any glance in her direction would back her up, make her cautious. In her growing anxiety, she had moved out of the shadows. Close enough for me to make my move.

Still facing the amazon woman, I made one more cautious revolution around the circle. When I knew that the blonde was only a few feet directly behind me, I made a fake lunge toward Misty, then twisted low and knocked the revolver from the blonde's grasp with the cutting edge of my right hand. I had my weight behind it, guessing distance and angle, and when I hit her arm there was the dry-twig *kerWHACK* of the carpus bones bursting in her right wrist.

"Damn . . ."

It brought Misty in on a charge, nunchakus cutting the air above my head. It was no time to play her karate games. I truthfully didn't care if she was better than I, or if I was better than she. I just wanted to get the hell off that island.

I dove low in an effective crack-back block, and felt the weight of her come down on top of me. Oh, she was strong—for a woman; stronger, in fact, than most men. But I had sixty pounds on her and considerably more bulk. I slid from beneath her, rolled, and then pinned her, back to the ground. The blonde still sat on the ground, holding her wrist and moaning.

"Hold still, damn it."

"I'll kill you!" She spit furiously at my face.

"Misty, I don't want to hurt you. Now just co-operate and I won't have to."

I got her up off the ground and located the revolver. The blonde was crying like a homesick kid. I felt sorry for both of them.

"Your time will come, pretty boy!"

"I know, Misty. It comes for us all."

I forced them into the root cellar. The amazon clawed and scratched. She took a sizable chunk of my left hand with her. And I was just about to slam and lock the door behind them when I thought of something. I had hurt the tall one enough. I had no desire to burden her with anything more.

"Misty—about your friend, Mary Sue . . . ? I was lying."

I got a screeching hiss in return. "You *bastard!*"

I trotted over to the squat generator building and kicked away the makeshift crossbar. The Irishman sat comfortably on the dirt floor in an angle of moonlight. He looked up when I came in.

"What took ye so long, Yank?" he asked non-chalantly.

"Ran into some heavy traffic."

He got up and brushed off his pants. "Wouldn't expect that on an island sech as this, now would ye?"

"Westy, do you know how to hot-wire a car engine?"

He looked almost offended. "An' what good Irish lad doesn't? The Protestants are very fussy about leavin' their keys in their automobiles."

"Good. Get down to the Shamrock. It's got the basic Ford two-bolt starter. Be careful no one sees you. I'll be down by the time you have it going."

"Have ta stop an' see a friend, I suppose."

"Not a friend," I said.

I turned to go, but the Irishman stopped me. "Dusky, lad, I found somethin' very interestin' in that wee building. Got so bored waitin' on ye that I did a bit a rummagin' around—lookin' for a weapon, ye might say. But all I found was this—inside one of them oil drums, it was."

He held something up in the light. I took it, squinting to see what it was.

"American dollars, Yank," O'Davis said. "Stacks of 'em. An' all soakin' wet with salt water. . . ."

14

I slipped quietly through the shadows.

The green numerals of my Rolex said there wasn't much time until dawn: four-thirty a.m.

Mahogany Key still slept, bathed in June moonlight. Something rattled in the bushes, and I came to an abrupt halt, my breath coming soft and low, my heart pumping audibly within my chest.

A raccoon came loping into the moonlight. Its back was hunched up, as if it ran on tiptoes. It stopped when it saw me, more indifferent than frightened.

"So, how's the hunting, partner?"

The coon's yellow eyes studied me intently.

"Well, if it's any consolation, I haven't had the best of luck either."

The coon gave me another long look, then rambled back off into the shadows.

I had kept the short-barreled Model 60. The walnut grip tucked into my khaki pants was abrasive against my belly flesh.

The big wooden building where Saxan kept her office loomed before me. There were no lights within, but the windows were silver glazed in the reflection of the moon.

I mounted the porch, wood creaking beneath my weight. As I expected, the door was locked. But the windows were open, covered only by screens. Quietly, I slipped out one of the frames and stepped through.

The room still smelled of old wood and of the musky perfume that Saxan used. It filled me with an odd sense of loss.

"Some people you feel as if you had always known. . . ."

And sometimes you're dead wrong.

There was a kerosene lamp on one of the tables. I found matches and lighted it. There was an almost military sterility about Saxan's metal desk. I tested the drawers, knowing they would be locked, then got down on my stomach and found the screwbolt on the bottom of the file cabinet. I had to lift the desk to remove the rod that held the drawers shut.

I didn't want to leave Mahogany Key emptyhanded.

I wanted something to take with me, some evidence more concrete than the soggy stacks of twenties the Irishman had found.

Holding the kerosene lamp, I went through the

files. I removed the folders on Barbara and Misty. But there were none on Saxan or Ms. Abhner. I stuffed the two folders down my shirt and continued my search.

The bogus account ledger was easy enough to find. It was in the top drawer: a green hardback book with a steel brace for a spine. In neatly inked entries were kept incoming and outgoing monies; the amount of donations and an equal amount of government matching funds. It was the one she would show to government inspectors. Not the one I was looking for.

The other—the real one—had to be somewhere. I stood thinking, hands on hips. Whatever she was, Saxan was a scientist first; a person driven to keep precise records. And she would keep that record book handy. But where?

And that's when it hit me: *I'm afraid the only thing I've had published was my master's thesis. And it wasn't exactly a best seller. . . .*

It was worth a try.

Carrying the lamp, I went to the broad bookshelf by the window. It took me a while to find it, but I did: a flat, thin volume lying down behind some other books.

Benefits of Mobility in Calliactis tricolor *(the Tricolor Anemone).* By Saxan Benton.

A perfect subject for someone like Saxan. The sea anemone is wildly beautiful to the eye, but it retracts and disappears at the first touch.

And it can sting.

I opened the book. The figures I was looking for were neatly kept on a sheath of blank pages. The women of Mahogany Key had been taking in a lot of money lately.

One hell of a lot of money.

In the last eleven months, Saxan had made five very large entries. She had figured percentages, salaries, and expenses. The last large entry she had made was June 22—the day after the *Blind Luck* had gone up in flames.

"Find what you're looking for, Dusky?"

In one swift motion, I pulled the .38 out of my belt, whirled, and landed belly first on the bare wooden floor, revolver aimed at the voice.

"Go ahead and shoot, Dusky. That's what Sam Spade would do, isn't it? Okay, you've cracked the case. Now it's time to shoot the bad guy. Do I look like a bad guy, Dusky?" A weary smile crossed her face. "Well, maybe that's because I am."

It was Saxan.

She stood in the doorway, her face illuminated by the moon.

For the first time, she wore her hair down. It lay over her shoulders, long and silken, the auburn softness turned to rust-blond by the light.

She wore a long translucent robe, oddly oriental.

And very obviously, she wore nothing underneath.

I got slowly to my feet, still holding the .38. It

felt ridiculous to keep a gun pinned on a woman I had wanted to take as a lover only a few hours earlier.

But I've felt ridiculous before, so I kept the revolver at hip level. Ready.

"You're up late. Or is it that you just got up early?" I said.

She closed the door quietly behind her, and came close enough for me to smell the perfume she wore. "Are you trying to account for my whereabouts at the time of the crime? Or is it that you're really interested, Dusky?"

"You can cut out the detective stuff, Saxan. I'm not in the mood."

She came a step closer, an arm's length away. In the corona of lamplight, I could see her face clearly: perfect nose and skin, the flawless contours made even more captivating by the strange off-center eyes. It was a different Saxan Benton who stood before me now. She was no longer the aristocrat with a vulnerable core. Awash with her guises, her own uncertainty, it seemed as if she had abandoned them all, and now stood exposed to her own eyes. And it didn't seem as if she liked what she saw.

"But aren't you a detective, Dusky? Isn't that the role you're playing? You know—sniff out the facts; solve the case?" She reached into the pocket of her robe, hesitated when I lifted the .38, then went ahead, a strange smile on her face.

"Cigarette?" she said.

"No thanks."

She bent over the kerosene lamp, then exhaled without inhaling, holding the cigarette in her right hand, elbow bent. "I don't smoke either. Funny, huh? But I decided this was a good night to start. I had this professor in college who had a theory about smoking. He said that when all those facts about cigarettes causing cancer came out, people started smoking because they had repressed suicidal tendencies. Do you believe that, Dusky?"

"I've had enough of your boomerang talk—that's just about exactly what I believe."

"Ready for a few straight facts, huh?"

"That's right, Saxan."

"Sam Spade would be proud, Dusky."

She walked across the room, switched on the desk light, then lay back on the couch. She crossed her legs, pulling the robe up to her thighs. "Here, does this fit the scene better? But I should be a dishwater blonde, right?" Her eyes were troubled, glassy, like someone teetering on the edge. "And sexually, I guess I should be a little more . . . conventional. But at least I have the cigarette!"

I went over to her quickly, took her arm, and shook her lightly.

"Damn it, Saxan, that's enough. Snap out of it!"

Her eyes grew wide, her mouth trembled, and then she fell back on the couch, wilting in her own tears. The sobs came in long swells of anguish, wracking her whole body. I pulled her close and held her.

"Maybe it's not as bad as you think, Dusky."

"And maybe it's worse than you think, Saxan."

She pulled away from me, smoothed the robe down, and wiped her eyes. She sniffed and looked into my eyes sadly. "So this is where you tell me how you have it figured, right? Let's hear the facts, Sam. I'll correct you when you're wrong."

I had been holding her hand. I released it, letting it fall back into her lap. "Okay. Fine, Saxan. You know, you really got to me—you did. Sure, you're very beautiful, and you're very intelligent and all, but there was something else about you that attracted me. I mean, you really had me; really took me in—"

"Just the facts, Sam! . . . please."

She had that wild, teetering look again. "The facts, Saxan? Okay, how's this? You get all involved with this feminist group, SELF. Now this little group isn't like most feminist organizations. This group is made up of honest to God man-haters. Like that little gem Misty, who tried to knock my head off about twenty minutes ago. And Barbara."

"Barbara?"

"That's right, Barbara. But I'm getting ahead of myself. I mean, you want the whole investigation laid out for you, right? Okay, so these women are not only man-haters, they're lesbians. That makes things very comfy and very damn private. So one of your people—that Abhner dame, probably—comes up with this wild scheme. The government has this island in Florida available to qualified organizations. Well, SELF qualifies, but you know you can't come up with the matching funds it takes to run a place like this. I mean, it is expensive, right?"

"Extremely expensive, Dusky."

"So you notice there's a lot of drugrunning going on down here. And all you have to do is read the newspapers to know that the big-time drugrunners carry one hell of a lot of money aboard. Sometimes as much as a half million, and it's all in cash. And it's safe cash, too—stuff the IRS boys have never heard of. So you put your little heads together and figure out a way to get it. First you have to bait them in. You stick some half-naked charmer like Barbara on a beach—"

"That's not true!"

"—and she's carrying just the right amount of explosives. Women can learn how to be carpenters and plumbers—you said that yourself. Explosives would be a snap for someone like you. Once the charge is set, the chick bails out. She always carries a lifejacket so she can make it to shore. Then you hire some goons to search the wreck for you. They use mullet nets and scuba gear. The drug boys invariably hide their loot in the bilge. It sinks fast while the rest of the boat burns. It probably takes awhile to find the money, but you do okay. . . ."

"Dusky, you're wrong about—"

I took her arms and shook her again. "Damn it,

you wanted the facts, so now I'm giving them to you!" She sat back wearily on the couch, resigned to listen. "But you had some problems after blowing up the *Blind Luck*. You didn't get to Barbara first. We did. And you learned enough from her to know we might be hooked up with some kind of law-enforcement agency. It put a real cramp in your style. How were you going to bring back your pontoon boat and unload the money with us around? We'd probably be asleep—but you couldn't take that chance, could you, Saxan?" I watched her closely now as I spoke; watched the words hit her—and the words seemed to hurt. "So you made a little visit to my bed in the infirmary—"

"Oh God, Dusky, you're so wrong. . . ."

"And you arranged to have someone else visit Westy."

She put her hands in her face, crying now.

"You really had me, Saxan. I fell for your cock-and-bull story. And you know what really hurts? You still have me—that's the kind of idiot I am. I thought that night really meant something."

"It did!" She stood up, near hysterics. "Dammit, Dusky, it meant everything! No, you listen for a minute! Just shut up and listen!" She pulled the robe tight around her neck, trembling in the hot June night. "You're wrong about Barbara. You're wrong about all of our women. Sure, some of them are homosexual. And there are even a couple of sickos like Misty and her friends, who would do anything Ms. Abhner told them to do. But the rest of the women aren't involved at all, Dusky! It's only me—can't you understand that? Eleven months ago, this woman I'd never met before came to me. Her name was Gloria Abhner. She was very cryptic, that first meeting, but she made it clear she had come up with a way to make a great deal of money. I was interested, of course. As you said, running this island is very expensive. We were about to lose the place—and after all the hard work we'd put into it!"

"So you naturally gave in, right?" I said. "After all, you wouldn't have to kill *that* many people—and only men—"

"Damn it, Dusky, can't you just listen for a minute?" She took me by the shoulders when she said it, eyes pleading, hurt.

"Okay," I said. "Go ahead."

She stood up and began to pace before me. "This woman said that what *we* would be doing would not be illegal—that we would be required only to hold and then transport certain articles to the mainland for her. For that, she said, we would be well paid."

"And you agreed?"

"No. Can you believe that? Well, I didn't. It was very obvious to me that what *she* would be doing *was* illegal. And I couldn't take the chance of getting SELF involved, because, no matter what you think, Dusky, it is a very worthwhile organization.

So I politely declined, said goodbye to her, and thought that was the end of it."

"But it wasn't?"

She shook her head. "No, I'm sorry to say it wasn't. I began to get unsigned letters. But it was pretty obvious who they were from. They were threatening letters. Blackmail, you might say." She looked at me, that strange sadness in her eyes. "Do you know what would happen, Dusky, if, say, the Miami *Herald* came out with a story about how the government is underwriting an island full of homosexuals?" She snapped her fingers. "The public outcry would close us down like *that*. So, she had us. I finally agreed—with the understanding that we would only act as a clearing house for whatever in the hell she had planned."

"You never knew?"

She chuckled sourly. "I'm a very bright woman, remember, Dusky? I figured it out after she blew up the first boat. But then she *really* had us. Don't you see? We were accomplices to murder, then. All of us! Every woman here—even though I was the only one to know what was going on. Ms. Abhner recruited Misty and a couple of others on her own. The sickos stick together, you see."

She fell back on the couch wearily and took my hand. It was the gesture of someone being swept away by despair. I squeezed the hand and noticed that she squeezed back.

"But why Mahogany Key, Saxan? Why was this

Abhner dame so desperate that you help? Why
not just work the whole scam on her own?"

She shrugged. "I've thought about that. You
see, she needed someone with an unimpeachable
public base to move the money. But, better than
that, she had a tax-exempt organization in us. Big
donations from private sources are commonplace.
A lot of wealthy people like to remain anonymous
when they make large donations. It was a perfect
way for her to launder the money back into legiti-
mate use."

"Barbara wasn't involved at all?"

She shook her head. "Absolutely not. I don't
know who was actually finding the boats and setting the charges. I suppose it was those horrible
fishermen—but you see now, don't you, why I
couldn't turn them in to the authorities?" She took
a deep breath and shuddered. "What happened
to Barbara was one of the unexpected tragedies.
And God knows, there have been enough of those
around here lately." She turned to me then,
reached up and touched my face. "But one thing
I want you to know, Dusky. I want you to know
that when I came to you that night it was because
I wanted to. It was because, suddenly, you made
me care so much that—"

"How very sweet. And how very disgusting!"

I reached for the .38 and found nothing. It glim-
mered on the desk beneath the light where I had
left it when I went to Saxan. And I knew then that

it was over; knew that whatever she had wanted to say to me would now be left unfinished.

In the doorway stood the rotund figure of Ms. Gloria Abhner.

And in her meaty right hand was a 9mm Parabellum. . . .

15

The Parabellum is a singularly brutal-looking handgun.

It's also—and usually incorrectly—called a German Luger.

Whatever she called it, this Ms. Abhner held it as if she knew how to use it. She obviously had a taste for fine weaponry.

"What a sweet little scene you two have been playing," she said in her froggish voice. She motioned at Saxan. "And I had such confidence in your . . . how should I say this? Your taste in lovers."

"Shut up!" Saxan yelled wildly. She made a lurching step toward the old woman, but I caught her and pulled her back. She wasn't crying now. She was furious. "Haven't you already done your best to ruin my life? If you're going to kill us, kill us. But don't torment me any more, you . . . you bitch!"

Abhner walked slowly from the door to the desk and picked up the .38. She studied it momentarily, then slipped it into the pocket of her baggy dress. She still wore the floppy, wide-brimmed hat—a ludicrous sight in light of the weapon she held.

"I was most distressed to find Misty and her friend locked away," she said. "They were rather upset about it. Killing mad, you might say. They are hunting your Irish friend down right now, Mr. MacMorgan. And they'll take no foolish chances this time. They're armed—"

Just as the words left her mouth, the sound of gunfire echoed through the morning darkness. A smile creased her face.

"Ah," she said. "That would be them now. And since your friend was unarmed—isn't that right?—I think we may safely assume that he is quite dead."

I forced my voice to be steady. "You're wrong, lady. He was armed. And I imagine he's on his way up here right now."

It was a lie. And she wasn't about to go for it. "No, I think not, Mr. MacMorgan. A nice try, but I know better. You were both carefully frisked, remember?" She patted the pocket of her dress. "And this is my revolver."

"So what are you going to do with us?"

Standing in the shadows now, her body mimed surprise. "Why, kill you, of course! It's all arranged, you see. I'll have your boat within the next few hours. Then I'll just tap you on the head, run you out a couple of miles, and set the correct charge."

She made an exploding motion with her hands. "Just one more boat dynamited, you see? The authorities will assume the drugrunners are at war again—and that you just happened to get in the way."

I had to keep her talking; had to give myself time to think, to come up with a plan. "So you were the one setting the charges? But how? Why would they let you aboard? Those guys are suspicious of everyone—especially some old dame—"

"I have my methods," she said cryptically. "I have my ways."

And that's when I knew; knew for the first time that my earliest suspicions—abandoned after Saxan's confession—were correct.

But I never got a chance to confront Abhner with it.

And she never got a chance to say another word to me.

At that moment, my wild Irish friend, Westy O'Davis, came crashing through the door. There was an odd expression on his face—almost as if he was enjoying himself. I noticed that he was bleeding from the nose, and that his dark shirt was soaked with something.

"I'll shoot them both!"

The figure in the hat spun to fire, but the Irishman ducked under the handgun, head low, shoulders wide, and hit her with a force that would have snapped the neck of any normal human being.

"Saxan—jump behind the couch!"

She didn't have to. Even as I said it, I was lifting her up and dumping her safely behind it.

I ran across the room and picked up the Parabellum.

I could have stopped them. And I almost did. But O'Davis still had that crazy look of delight on his face; an Irishman's delight in a two-fisted, no-holds-barred fight.

They seemed to be evenly matched for a while. Saxan's desk toppled beneath their weight. And then the bookcase came down. I grabbed the kerosene light, holding it up for safety—and to make sure the .38 didn't reappear from the dress pocket.

Finally, O'Davis ended the fight with a series of crashing right hands to the head. The figure in the dress lay on the floor, still breathing. The hat was gone. And so was the wig.

The Irishman climbed unsteadily to his feet. He looked offended. "I'd like ta thank ye fer the help, Yank! Was it that ye wanted ta see this creature beat the devil out o' me?"

"You're a growing boy," I said. "You need your exercise."

I studied the blood on his shirt. "Did Misty and her friend shoot you?"

"Me? Hah! The likes o' them shootin' me—now that is somethin' ta smile about. Didn't even have ta hurt them, I didn't. They're tied up down at the quay, they are."

"So where did the blood come from?"

He touched his nose gingerly. He looked almost embarrassed. "Ah . . . well . . . the tall one may have got one good lick in—but I was off my guard!" He moved his nose from side to side. "Lord o' saints, I think the nasty woman may o' broken me fine face."

"Join the club," I said.

Saxan came crawling out from behind the couch. There was a look of shock upon her face. She walked slowly to where her Ms. Gloria Abhner lay unconscious. "My God," she said, "it's not even a . . ." She looked at me, incredulous.

I bent down over the body, checking pulse and pupils. The rank smell of cigar smoke was strong on the dress, and the makeup didn't help anymore.

"It's Chief Petty Officer Spears, United States Coast Guard," I said.

16

It was the anniversary of our country's independence: a calm July morning, and the sea around my Calda Bank piling house was a sheen of turquoise clear to the horizon, soft and swollen, like a mirage. It was one of those uncommonly clear days. Pelicans wheeled and crashed, feeding in the distance. And you could see fish moving over the bottom through the water a long way off.

I stood by the rail on my rickety wooden porch, enjoying it all. It was going to be a hot day, but there was a freshness to the heat, and the sun felt good on bare chest and legs. I slipped back inside, cracked open an icy Tuborg, tapped the first dip of Copenhagen between cheek and gum, then went back outside to watch the Irishman.

He had left three days earlier in the Whaler, a sly-dog expression on his face.

It was an expression I had come to know well; a look that made me uncomfortable.

"Now look, O'Davis," I had said. "If you're going to go in town and cat around on your own—that's one thing. In fact, I wish you luck. But if you're going ashore with any idea of surprising me—"

"Brother MacMorgan, please! Give me a little credit, me boy. Was it not meself who saved yer life?"

"Oh, Lord. . . ."

"Fer what was it? The third time? Aye." He had his hands on his hips, that leprechaun expression on his face. "I've saved yer shabby life *three* times, an' now ye have the nerve ta lecture me! Can't ye see, lad, that I only have yer best interest in mind?"

"Do I have to hear this again?"

"Like those fine little oriental folk say: you save a man's life, an' yer responsible fer that life." He clapped me on the shoulder. "So ya see, Yank, it's only fer a little recreation that I'm goin' inta Key West. That an' rent a wee small sailboat so as not to lose me touch at the tiller."

The "wee small sailboat" O'Davis had rented was a thirty-two-foot Morgan, booms fore and aft under full canvas. It was painted a bright yellow, and, I noted wryly, there wasn't enough wind, so he had its little diesel engine revved up, puttering the sleek windship along.

I took a sip of the cold Tuborg and watched

him move it expertly along the marker maze of Calda Bank.

On one count, the Irishman was right—he did deserve a little recreation. Our vacation in the Ten Thousand Islands had turned into a complete bust after we notified the authorities and had Chief Spears and his goons rounded up. We had spent the next two days making sworn testimonies on the little tape recorders the federal boys brought with them. And when I had time—which wasn't often between the question sessions—I visited Saxan in the sterile Naples jail where she was being temporarily held.

"I can't believe you're still interested, Dusky, after all that's happened."

"Loyalty is one of my few virtues, Saxan."

"Even if I go to prison?"

And I had laughed. *"Your lawyer says there's absolutely no danger of that. The blackmail letters, remember? You were smart enough to keep them. And Chief Spears was stupid enough to use his own handwriting. . . ."*

It was, in truth, the only mistake Spears had made. I had to give him credit—he had worked the whole scam almost perfectly. As a Coast Guard officer, he could board any boat at will. Not even the men in his watch suspected when, in his cursory inspections, he left just the right amount of explosives behind. Then, disguised as Ms. Gloria Abhner, he was free to set up his own private collection agency.

The aging officer, making a desperate stab at wealth and retirement, had the drugrunners coming and going.

I had suspected him only briefly—when Barbara told me how the *Blind Luck* had rendezvoused with some other unseen vessel. And what other boat was in those waters? My radar aboard *Sniper* had told me—only the Coast Guard's *Royal Palm.* But how could a whole Coast Guard crew be involved? That's what had stumped me and finally made me decide Barbara was lying. But she wasn't lying. The answer was simple: Spears's fellow Coasties didn't know. Even so, it had surprised the Irishman when I had asked Norm Fizer over the phone in Everglades City to check him out. In an organization as excellent as the United States Coast Guard, the thought of even one bad apple wounds them deeply.

So I watched the Irishman weave his pretty windship on toward my piling house. When he got close enough, he waved gaily and yelled, "Brung ye a little surprise, Yank!"

And that's exactly what I had been afraid of. I went back inside cursing softly, and returned wearing a pair of shorts.

"O'Davis, you maniac! You're a menace to yourself and everyone who knows you."

"Hah! Is that true, now?" He sat at the helm holding a half-empty bottle of Irish whiskey. He was sunburned, bare-chested, and his red hair and beard were in wild disarray. "An' we were about ta invite ye ta join us tonight in watchin' the Key West fireworks from this fine pretty ship.''

He held the Morgan off my piling house expertly, close enough for me to see inside the little cabin; close enough to see that he wasn't alone.

''Not tonight, Westy. Just want to spend a quiet evening alone tonight, thanks.''

''But ye haven't seen who I've brung, Yank!''

And that's when the girl came topside, hair like white spun glass, ripe body covered in the barest of string bikinis.

''Barbara!''

''Goddamn right, Dusky!'' She stood tanned and grinning, more beautiful than I had ever seen her.

But then my joy in seeing her was suddenly overcome by something else. ''Barbara, it was really sweet of you to come out here to keep me company. But I'm afraid that I . . . ah . . . do want to be alone.''

The girl looked suddenly embarrassed, while the Irishman's face showed puzzlement—and then amusement. He said, ''An' ye say I'm conceited, Yank! Now that is a laugh!'' And in answer to my own look of puzzlement, he explained, ''Yank, don't ye see? Barbara's me folk singer! The one I stayed with on the island. She's with me! We're jest wonderin' if ye'd like ta share our company tonight.''

And suddenly, I felt very good. The awkward situation I had feared was no longer awkward. I made them promise to come back after the Fourth of July display. I said that we would eat fresh fish and drink cold beer, and that they could sing some of the songs they had been practicing.

They both thought that was funny.

And when they were gone, safely puttering away across the turquoise expanse of sea, the woman came out. She wore only one of my soft blue cotton shirts. It was not buttoned, and her small firm breasts thrust the material away, showing the sweet soft line of stomach, the belly button, and the flaxen curl between thighs. She put her arms around me, whispering in my ear.

"You turned those nice people down?"

"Hmmm . . . well, it seemed like the thing to do."

"They were my friends, too, Dusky. And it is Independence Day, you know—I thought you were more patriotic than that."

I turned to meet her kiss, feeling lips hot and moist, mouth opening as my hand moved up her body to touch the perfect breasts.

"Doesn't this seem patriotic?"

"Oh . . . it does . . . yes . . . should I salute that?"

"Haven't I taught you anything, woman? It's hardly for saluting."

And Saxan Benton giggled. "Guess that means I need another lesson, huh? My professors always said I was a slow learner, Dusky. But once I learn, I never forget. . . ."

Here's an exciting glimpse of the thrilling adventure that awaits you in the next novel of this action-packed series:

THE ASSASSIN'S SHADOW

I agreed to become an assassin one blustery wind-leached day in a Florida March.

Blustery isn't even the word for it. Those of you who live in America's northlands don't hear much about the bad weather—and it's not because we don't have our share of it. The Sunshine State's chambers of commerce become meterological gestapos when the skies pale and the winds blow foul. It's not the sort of thing they paste on Indiana billboards, or promote in double-truck ads in *The Times.* You can see it on the faces of Florida's TV weathermen. Their smiles are vaguely apologetic, and their eyes dart between storm fronts like unfaithful husbands confessing they have contracted an unexpected case of genital herpes. Transplants in Florida consider bad weather an affront, and to fellow tourists they aim silly, accusing barbs like: "Ya' musta brought the cold with ya' when ya' flew down. . . ."

And as winters go, this had been one of the worst. Cold front after cold front funneled down from the Midwest, roiling the seas with careening winds. The white board shipbuilders' houses on Duval and Elizabeth Streets stayed shuttered, and the smell of woodsmoke from the rare fireplace drifted across the pirate streets of Key West, off and on, all winter long. There were the brief winter weeks of 80-degree temperatures. But just when you thought the bad weather was gone for good, holed up someplace in Ohio where it justly belonged, the blue northers would rage again through the palms and eucalypti, and those of us on charterboat row would cluster around mugs of hot coffee at the Kangaroo's Pouch and eye our empty boats sourly.

As Captain Gainey Maxwell of the *Lookout II* put it one bleak January morning, "Boys, I've come ta' believe that the only thing that stands between Key West and the winds a' Canada is a piddly line of mangroves and a barbed wire fence someplace in Iowa."

It was that kind of winter.

And when the seas are eight to ten feet outside the reef, there isn't much for a bluewater fishing guide to do. It didn't bother me as much as it did some of the others. They had wives and kids and mortgages to worry about. But not me—not any longer. My family, my world, had been wiped out in another lifetime. The drug pirates had seen to that. Balmy summer nights in the tropics are for love and long walks and—for little boys—time to play with their adoring father. Murderers don't plant ignition bombs in cars when the nights are star-blazed and the winds blow sweet and warm out of Cuba, and explosions don't scatter bits of the well-loved across lawns and vacation sidewalks.

It just doesn't happen. Not on balmy summer nights, it doesn't.

And the winters in Florida are never, ever cold. *Right . . .*

So I was alone, alone in a volatile winter—my first in the little house built on stilts a mile from the nearest land in the shallow water off Calda Bank. The house had been built to ice-store fish until the lighter boats could get around and pick them up for transport into Key West. Now, fifty years later, I had converted it to a bachelor home—as close as I could get to living in the sea that I loved, and as far away from the memories of Key West as I could manage without leaving altogether.

On that blustery March day I was suffering a case of the blahs. Too much wind and too much cold weather, and much too little exercise. I had awakened as always just before first light. A black north wind was rattling the windows and seeping through the cracks in the floor. Beneath my double bed I could hear a nasty cross chop washing around the pilings, and the strange gray light beyond the window told me it would be another rainy dawn. I shook off the urge to crawl back under the covers and sleep the morning away.

I had been sleeping too many mornings away. When the winds blow foul, you don't charter. And lately, with charters canceled, I had been doing a damn good impression of the typical suburban male animal who thinks boredom can be cured by eating too much and drinking too much, and wallowing in the gray confines of his own despair.

It's a cycle as easy to fall into as it is vicious. The longer you put off the training program, the diet, and the mental discipline, the easier it is to forget how the human machine is supposed to feel—how brain and body are supposed to harmonize in the fail-safe routine of hard work tempered with such well-deserved luxuries as cold beer.

And the moment you forget is the moment you are lost. You become only a dull brain governing the flabby remnant of your own humanity. The only place those two chubby legs are going to carry you is toward a rest home rendezvous.

And I wasn't about to let it go that far.

I threw back the brace of wool, Navy-issue blankets. The boards of the stilthouse floor were cold against my bare feet. In the weak dawn light, I nursed the squat Franklin stove to flame, then put coffee on to boil. Outside, March clouds scudded beneath stars in the waning darkness. Across Florida Bay, beyond Miami, the coming sun was a leached white, and slate waves feathered beyond my dock.

I finished urinating and walked down the rickety stairs to where my thirty-four-foot charterboat, *Sniper*, was moored. Damn it, if it was going to be another nasty day in Florida, for once I was going to face it head-on. Naked, I forced myself not to shiver. This was the day I would jerk myself out of the rut. How long had I been letting myself go? My Irish friend, Westy O'Davis, had left months ago for the Caymans, where—when he wasn't playing secret service agent for the United Kingdom—he passed the days teaching pretty tourist ladies how to scuba dive. And then that beautiful woman, that fine person, Saxan Benton, had finally written me off as a hopeless loner and returned north to pursue her botany studies. It was what the soap opera people might term an inadequate parting scene. . . .

"Dusky, you know why I'm leaving. I have my own life to think about. . . ."

"I know."

"And I have the feeling that, no matter how much you might come to love me, you would still be tied to your past."

"I know."

The lovely model's face had twisted, her composure shattered, and a trembling hand had brushed auburn hair away. "Damn it, don't just stand there like a dumb hulk! You know I care for you. You know I'd rather stay, if you could just . . . just . . .

Damn it, Dusky, do you understand what I'm trying to say!"

"I understand, Saxan. The boat's ready. I'll take you back to Key West now."

So I had spent the winter alone. People call it boredom, but it's really self-pity. I had taken some strange masochistic joy in eating too much and drinking too much, watching myself get slack and slow. When the damnable wind settled enough, I chartered, as always, out of Garrison Bight. And when the northers set in, I retreated to my stilt-house upon the sea to read and listen to night voices around the world on my transoceanic shortwave . . . and mope.

I had made some false starts getting back into shape. Those are danger signals—when you start, then allow yourself to stop. A Texas friend of mine named Treadwell has a saying: If you can't profit from adversity, then you damn well deserve to suffer.

Now was the time to end my winter suffering.

The March wind that dawn had a razor edge to it. I stood, hands on bare hips, facing it. Half a mile away, I could see the fitful blinking of the white four-second navigation marker off Fleming Key. There was a gray corona of light haloing Key West, then tailing away eastward along the over-seas highway like a comet's tail. My hands tugged experimentally at the fat I had let settle on stomach and sides. I hacked, spit with disgust, then went back inside and poured myself a mug of black coffee. I use a fifty-fifty mix of espresso and regular grind. I drank it quickly, burning the sleep, the fogginess, the laziness away.

Today's the day, MacMorgan. You've gorged yourself and slept the winter away. Now winter's over, no matter what that bastard northwind says. One more false start and you may never start again. . . .

The roof of my stilthouse is covered with tin and braced with stout Florida heart pine. I washed my coffee mug, put it away neatly. I took a deep breath, then jumped up and grabbed the middle beam. When I'm in shape, when I have my weight down to two-o-five, I can do thirty-six back-handed pull-ups. When you spend your boyhood in the circus, working the trapeze two shows a day—plus a morning practice session—your shoulders and arms develop a lot faster than your vocabulary. But I wasn't in shape now. And I was twenty pounds over my best weight. I huffed and puffed and trembled and shook, and twenty-one pull-ups was the best I could do.

Disgustedly, I jerked a towel from the shelf and went outside to *Sniper*, mopping my face.

Damn it, MacMorgan, you may have let it go too long this time. Maybe that's what you really want to be: just one more overweight, middle-aged American; just one more flaccid face in the crowd. . . .

I reached above the wheel and the chrome gleam of twin throttles and snapped on my new Horizon VHF. Channel sixteen was as empty as the March dawn.

"*Fred Astaire, Fred Astaire*, this is the charterboat *Sniper*, Whiskey, Foxtrot, Lima 7739, over."

I gave it two minutes, then repeated the call. Finally, the VHF answered me: "Vessel calling the *Fred Astaire*, this is the *Fred Astaire*. Channel sixty-eight, Dusky?"

"Switching six-eight."

I could picture Steve Wise aboard his floating hulk of a houseboat, *Fred Astaire*. He's dockmaster at my marina, and a popular man with the tourist ladies around Key West. When he's not having a party, he's usually enjoying a more private form of entertainment. More than one vacationing Midwesterner has caught the flight out of Key West with a flush on her face and a smile on her lips. And frankly, I felt kind of bad about waking Steve Wise up so early.

He didn't seem too pleased about it either. After we had both switched channels, he said, "Dusky, old buddy, old pal, it's not quite six a.m. by the lady's wristwatch I can see on the counter by this VHF. I hope you have a good reason for calling me out of my warm bed a full hour before I have to start dealing with the rest of the crazy charter boat captains . . . over."

"Steve, you'd have a dull life without us, and you know it."

"Yeah? Well, the young blonde who sleeps yonder in my master stateroom has been begging me to give it a try. She wants to stay aboard for the summer and go cruising across to the islands . . . over."

"And you don't have the heart to tell her that that floating strumpet parlor of yours doesn't have a healthy engine in it. Right?"

He was still chuckling as he transmitted. "Hey, keep your voice down. People monitor this channel. So what's your business, Captain? Now that I'm up, I don't see any sense in wasting the rest of the morning . . . over."

"Just wanted to officially cancel today's charter. Tell Dr. Taylor of Baltimore that we'll have to try it his next time through Key West. I'd have called you later, but I'm going to be busy. It's such a pretty day I'm going to go for a long swim . . . over."

"What? Oh yeah, sure Dusky, sure. Winds gusting to thirty knots, seas eight to ten feet, and you're going for a swim. Right. By the way, that bald friend of yours was at the marina yesterday. Said he wanted to see you. He must have got in touch, huh? Over."

I thought for a moment. My bald friend? It could be only one person—Colonel D. Harold Westervelt. And no, he hadn't gotten in touch with me. But if he had reason to see me he would—you could bet the bank on that. And he would have a damn good reason for seeing me. D. Harold doesn't leave his private orbit of discipline and work capriciously.

It could mean only one thing.

A mission. And if ever there was a time in my life when I wasn't fit for a mission, it was now.

"Yeah, that's right. He contacted me," I lied. "And if he stops back, Steve, tell him I'll be in touch." We chatted on a few minutes, trading good-natured barbs, and then signed off. I adjusted the squelch and turned the volume up full so that if someone tried to get in touch with me I could hear it in the house.

D. Harold Westervelt. We were similar by-products of two very, very different wars. His was the world conflict where men died for a reason. Mine was the Asian exercise in political lunacy where the mealymouthed fat cats used us as pawns. Still, neither of us had been able to leave our wars behind us. For years I thought that his only official capacity was that of weapons inventor for the United States military. Later, after the murder of my family had led to my being retained by a federal agency to help expedite its private wars, I learned that his unique genius was being used for much more than just unusual weaponry.

Even so, I was surprised that it was Colonel Westervelt who was trying to get in touch with me. My usual contact was an old acquaintance from Nam, one Stormin' Norman Fizer. I put the coffee pot on the little Franklin stove so it would stay hot as I thought about it. Why Westervelt? Why not Fizer, as it had been on the other missions? Did that mean it was more important—or less important? Or maybe it wasn't a mission at all; maybe D. Harold just wanted to say hello.

No, the key phrase was: "That bald friend of yours was at the marina."

And Colonel D. Harold Westervelt doesn't "just happen" to stop by anyplace. He plan his days of exercise and work like a human computer, allowing himself only a few well-loved recreations like classical music and growing orchids.

It had to be a mission.

Still naked, I strapped on my Randall attack-survival knife. A long swim at open sea is not without its hazards. Outside, the gray March wind blew the tops off waves. Frigate birds soared in the high distance, omens of a storm. I stood on the dock and looked out toward the blinking navigation light a half-mile away. That would be my destination—there and back. I did about five minutes of stretching, waiting for the sun. But it never arrived. Morning was to be a pallid slash to the east.

Another nasty winter's day in Vacation Land.

But at least I was facing this one head-on. And there was the promise of a mission. Later, I was sure, D. Harold would offer it to me in intricate, calculated detail. Infiltrate what, attack where, and maybe kill whom. It didn't matter. I'd accept. Because lately I'd been doing too good a job at slowly killing myself.

SIGNET

Randy Wayne White writing as Randy Striker

"Raises the bar of the action thriller."
—*Miami Herald*

KEY WEST CONNECTION

Ex-Navy SEAL Dusky MacMorgan survived a
military hell only to find it again where he least
expects it—as a fisherman trolling the Gulf
Stream in his thirty-foot clipper. His new life is
shattered when a psychotic pack of drug
runners turns the turquoise waters red with the
blood of his beloved family. Armed with an
arsenal so hot it could blow the Florida coast
sky-high, he's tracking the goons responsible—
right into the intimate circle of a
corrupt U.S. senator living beyond the law in his
own island fortress. But now it has to withstand
the force of a one-man hit-squad.

Available wherever books are sold or at
penguin.com